"The best of coal-town Pennsylvania in the midst of WWII, *Pieces of the Heart* offers a depiction of heartache and pain, determination and courage, and a vision of love in the thick of crisis and loss. This poignant story of a young lady's affection for her grandmother and love for a treasured pinecone prayer quilt and the man she'd fight to save at any cost will both compel and inspire you, even as your heart breaks at the portrayal of battered lives."
—Amber Stockton, historical fiction author of the Liberty's Promise and Brandywine Brides trilogies, and *Colonial Courtships*

"A fresh look at the World War II era, *Pieces of the Heart* reveals a slice of the African-American experience, from the appalling segregation of the US armed forces to the surprising discrimination within the black community. Cordelia and Bernard's love story is stitched on this historical background with colorful characters and fine craftsmanship. A story to treasure."
—Sarah Sundin, award-winning author of *With Every Letter*

"*Pieces of the Heart* from the Quilts of Love series captured my heart from page one. I loved the voice, the characters, the story . . . it was like I was living it with them. I couldn't put it down. Novel Rocket and I give it a high recommendation. It's a must read."
—Ane Mulligan, Senior Editor, Novel Rocket

"*Pieces of the Heart* does what I thought no book could do—provide fresh insight into World War II. Granted, the fact that the troops were segregated isn't news, but to "experience" it by climbing into the skin of the author's well-defined characters opens readers' eyes to the depth of struggles involved in that aspect of the conflict. Add to that a heart-tugging romance that begins in childhood and matures throughout the trials of moving into adulthood, as well as a unique twist on the battered-woman topic, and *Pieces of the Heart* will capture and enthrall readers from beginning to end."
—Kathi Macias, multi-award winning author of forty books, including *The Moses Quilt.*

"As a quilter and quilting teacher, I really am interested in this quilting series by Abingdon Press. Bonnie gave us a story that held my interest from the first word to the last one. I loved getting an insider's perspective of the lives of African Americans in World War II. Bonnie

took me straight into their hearts, and she shared the good, the bad, and the ugly. Sometimes the book wasn't an easy read because of that, but it carried the characters and the reader through spiritual growth and redemption. I think every Christian should read this one."
—Lena Nelson Dooley, award-winning author of *Maggie's Journey, Mary's Blessing, Catherine's Pursuit,* and *Love Finds You in Golden, New Mexico*

Other books in the Quilts of Love Series

Beyond the Storm
Carolyn Zane
(October 2012)

A Wild Goose Chase Christmas
Jennifer AlLee
(November 2012)

Path of Freedom
Jennifer Hudson Taylor
(January 2013)

For Love of Eli
Loree Lough
(February 2013)

Threads of Hope
Christa Allan
(March 2013)

A Healing Heart
Angela Breidenbach
(April 2013)

A Heartbeat Away
S. Dionne Moore
(May 2013)

Pattern for Romance
Carla Olson Gade
(August 2013)

Raw Edges
Sandra D. Bricker
(September 2013)

The Christmas Quilt
Vannetta Chapman
(October 2013)

Aloha Rose
Lisa Carter
(November 2013)

Tempest's Course
Lynette Sowell
(December 2013)

Scraps of Evidence
Barbara Cameron
(January 2014)

A Sky Without Stars
Linda S. Clare
(February 2014)

Maybelle in Stitches
Joyce Magnin
(March 2014)

PIECES OF THE HEART

Quilts of Love Series

Bonnie S. Calhoun

Abingdon Press fiction
a novel approach to faith

Nashville, Tennessee

Pieces of the Heart

Copyright © 2013 by Bonnie S. Calhoun

ISBN-13: 978-1-4267-5272-8

Published by Abingdon Press, P.O. Box 801, Nashville, TN 37202
www.abingdonpress.com

Published in association with Hartline Literary Agency.

Library of Congress Cataloging-in-Publication Data has been
requested.

Printed in the United States of America

1 2 3 4 5 6 7 8 9 10 / 18 17 16 15 14 13

To my father and mother, Wellington and Venis Jones. God rest both of your souls and thank you, Dad, for your service to your country and your WWII experiences on New Caledonia.

Acknowledgments

I want to thank my Abingdon team including my senior acquisitions editor, Ramona Richards; my editor on this book, Teri Wilhelms; marketing manager, Cat Hoort; and the rest of the great team at Abingdon, including Sales and Marketing, that made this book possible.

And special thanks go out to my agent, Terry Burns, for always believing in me; to all of my critique buddies in the Penwrights and Little Pennies; and to my personal editor, Angie Breidenbach. Thank you, Lord Jesus, for watching over me and bringing these special people into my life.

1

June 15, 1938

Corde-eel-ee, don't be sil-ly. We'll find you sooner or later!"

The taunt echoed down the alley, bouncing from building to building at the same rate her heartbeat pounded in her ears. The voices pumped more adrenaline into her blood. Would they pop into the Court from Pine Street?

Cordelia Grace pedaled her red and tan Schwinn as fast as her legs would go. She sucked in short, rapid breaths that burned her lungs. She took a glance behind. No one. She swerved, avoiding the metal garbage cans in front of Stoney's Garage. Panic raced through her throat as tears pricked at her eyes. Where were her two girlfriends? They were supposed to be right behind her. Now she was alone to face her tormentors.

She probably wouldn't have run from them if she had "more meat on her bones," like Grammy said. Other girls had the weight and power she lacked. Why did she have to fight? Truth be told, she didn't know *how* to fight. Her daddy was a preacher man, and her momma always said young ladies of good breeding didn't act like street hoodlums. No one had ever taught her self-defense.

She breathed hard, pulling in big gulps of air. Maybe they hadn't seen her turn down Dix Court? Maybe she could make it home safely . . . today. The alley, wide enough for cars to pass in either direction, felt as though it were closing in on her, squeezing her into the dusty center. She prayed someone would be on their porch. Just one grown-up she could stop and talk with until the danger passed. But each house stood silent, each narrow porch empty. Rows of garbage cans lined impossibly narrow strips of grass like tin soldiers, but none offered protection.

The quarter-sized scab on her left knee caught on the hem of her play dress as her legs pumped the pedals. The tiny prickle pains from the pulled skin would be worth it if she managed to escape. She jerked her head around to look back again. Her long, skinny braids whacked her in the face and slapped her in the right eye. Tears spilled onto her cheek. Bitsy Morgan's house marked the halfway point in the alley. Still no one in hot pursuit.

Her arms relaxed on the handlebars and her legs slowed. She back-pedaled to brake. The bicycle slid to a stop. Cordelia hopped off the seat and straddled the "J" frame. Her lungs burned.

Five houses up, they emerged on the path leading to the avenue. The three bullies spread across the Court, blocking her way.

Cordelia whimpered as dread clenched her belly. They had found her. She tried to turn, but the chain caught her dress hem, wrenching the handlebars from her grip. The bicycle fell, and the chain dug into the soft flesh of her ankle. A trail of black grease tracked down one of her white socks. *Ignore the pain. If they see tears, they'll know I'm scared.* She lifted her quivering chin and stared at them.

Two girls and a boy ran at her.

She bent over and raised her bicycle.

Two more girls raced toward her. The five Wilson kids had trapped their prey. She tried not to let fear register in her eyes.

"Cor-deel-lee, you belong to me." Debbie Lu, the tallest girl in the group, had her nappy hair scraped back in a short pony-tail so tight it pulled back the corners of her eyes, adding to her sinister look.

Cordelia shrank back, choking her handlebars with shaking hands. She watched the Wilson girl approach, slapping her fist into the palm of her other hand.

Debbie Lu charged and slammed into Cordelia with the full force of both fists.

Cordelia stumbled from her bicycle and skidded on the ground. Her palms raked over the graveled dirt of the alley. The sting forced tears into her eyes. She refused to respond.

A red flash streaked from the roof of the shed on the left side of the alley. A cute light-skinned boy landed on the ground beside her bicycle. He wore blue jeans and a bright red shirt opened down the front to reveal a dingy T-shirt. Cordelia eyed him warily—another tormentor?

He didn't join the bullies.

She looked him up and down. Who was he? Her heart pounding eased.

The cute boy stepped between her and Debbie Lu. "What's the problem?" He pointed his thumb back at Cordelia. "Did she steal your Tootsie Pop?"

"I'm gonna pop her, all right. Little Miss High Yella' doesn't belong in this neighborhood with her light skin and straight hair. She acts like she's white people and better'n us," said the dark-complexioned girl.

The cute boy turned away from Debbie Lu to glance at Cordelia.

Cordelia froze.

He raised one side of his lips in a slight smile and winked, then turned back to the menace. "In case you haven't noticed, you should probably call me high yella' too since my skin is as light as hers. Does that mean you want me out of the neighborhood, too?" He stepped closer to the girl. "See, I just moved here, and I don't think my pa would want to leave, since he just got a job at the coal company."

The girl scowled but lowered her fist and backed up.

Tim Wilson, one brother of the group, pushed Debbie Lu out of the way and stood toe-to-toe with the new boy. "Don't you talk to my sister like that."

"Or what?" The cute boy's eyebrows furrowed and he lowered his head a tad.

Cordelia eyed the exchange. Her brain told her to run while she had the chance, but her feet stayed rooted to the spot. What did he think he was doing, facing off with the Wilson kids? They were well-known scrappers.

Tim Wilson raised his left hand.

The cute boy's right fist shot out and punched Tim square in the nose.

Tim's hands cupped his nose as blood squirted down the front of his shirt and splattered his sisters.

The girls screamed and hightailed it down the alley.

Cordelia grimaced. An involuntary sigh pushed from her chest. This boy wasn't afraid of them.

"I'll get you for this," Tim warned in a nasal tone.

"Yeah, well, when you're not bleeding and wanna stop playing house with your sisters, be sure and let me know."

Tim pointed a bloody finger at the boy. "Hey, you take that back or I'm gonna beat your—"

"Oh, no! I'm sorry," the cute boy interrupted, his voice pleading. "I didn't mean to hurt you."

Cordelia's heart sank. So much for her fearless hero. She couldn't blame him, but somehow it felt worse than Debbie Lu's fist in her belly.

Which way should she run before Tim called his sisters back to finish the job?

The boy added, "Yeah, I'm sorry. I meant to hit your sister."

Tim scowled through the mess dripping from his chin. He sputtered, but before he could speak, Cordelia's rescuer faked a lunge. Tim recoiled with a girlish squeal and sprang after his sisters.

Cordelia's eyes widened as she stared at the back of the cute boy's head.

He turned to face her. "Do you talk?"

A nervous smile crossed her lips. Her dry throat croaked out the word "Yes." She swallowed hard and wet her lips. "Thank you for helping me." A flutter settled into her tummy.

He looked down at the splatter of blood on his own sleeve. With a look of disgust he ripped the shirt off and threw it to the ground. A rolled-up tube of paper fell from his back pocket. "Jeepers creepers, I gotta lose that. If my ma sees blood on my shirt, I'm gonna be in real big trouble for fightin' again."

Cordelia smiled. "I could explain for you. You were very brave—"

"No! Pa told me if I got in trouble in this town, he was gonna . . ." He kicked at the shirt then locked his fingers together over his head, resting his arms against his ears. "I'll run away before . . ."

Cordelia tipped her head to the side to look up into his downcast eyes. "Before what?"

He mumbled.

"What did you say?"

He looked defiant. "I said before I get beat again."

Cordelia jerked back her chin at the odd choice of words.

11

"Berr-nard!" A woman's voice carried over the fence.

"Com-ing," he yelled but never took his eyes off Cordelia.

His stare reached into her soul. She shivered. He looked about thirteen. Same age as her, but at least a head taller, and really cute. He'd be gone in a second. Cordelia's heart thumped an erratic rhythm. At least she knew his name . . . Bernard.

"I have to go before she comes looking for me. My dad will be home from the mines any minute. I got to already be at the dinner table when he comes in." He reached for the rickety wooden gate.

"Hey, you dropped something." Cordelia pointed at the rolled paper.

Bernard grabbed it up and unrolled the tube. Flattening the pages, he showed her the comic book with a mostly yellow and white cover. A man in blue tights and a red cape lifted a car over his head. "This is the first Action Comic! And this here is Superman. He flies over tall buildings."

Cordelia looked at the page, then back at Bernard. "So what?"

He just shook his head. "So what? Do you know how many extra chores I had to do for the ten cents to buy this?" He shook his head. "You're just a girl. Girls know nothin'."

She tipped her head to the side, and a smile creased her lips. "Well, can you fly and lift a car over your head?" He had used what she considered superhuman strength to save her. Her regular smart-alecky mouth displaced her anxiety. Grammy said her mouth always got her in trouble. She wanted to slap herself for being flippant.

He began to argue.

"Berr-nard, dinn-ner," the lady's voice yelled from the other side of the tall wooden fence.

He never took his eyes off Cordelia. "Comin', Ma!"

He turned to the gate, and then back to Cordelia. "What's your name, girl?"

"Cordelia . . . Cordelia Grace." Now her heart pounded for a different reason.

"Good to meet you, Cordelia-Cordelia Grace." He winked and reached for the gate.

"Welcome to the neighborhood." Cordelia's heart thumped against her ribs. Her voice trailed off as the gate closed behind him.

She leaned over and grabbed up the red shirt, then held it up, looking for spots of blood. Scrunching up her nose, she folded the splashes to the inside. Why did she want this dirty thing? She stuffed the shirt into the book bag in her bicycle basket, then pedaled out of the alley and down Olive Street.

May 19, 1942

"Did you hear what I asked you, baby girl?"

Cordelia's thoughts jerked back to the present, but her hand rested on the circle of red triangles. The memory both stung and warmed her heart. "I'm sorry. What did you ask, Grammy?"

"Well, I asked what had you deep in thought. You even breathed heavy for a spell there." Grammy Mae measured squares of colored cloth as she rocked in her chair.

Cordelia hitched up the side of her mouth in a wry smile. "You know how some people can pinpoint when their lives changed for the better or the worse?"

"Yes, baby. I've heard tell about folks like that. For me, I just personally felt it all began the day I was birthed." Grammy Mae, with her hair pulled back in a perfect chignon, wore a tailored housedress; she had looked prim and proper every day Cordelia could remember. Even her black Hill and Dale stack-heel oxfords were polished to a high shine. Grammy loved shoes. She had taught Cordelia the brand name of every pair, though, to her grandmother's chagrin, Cordelia preferred to go barefoot.

Cordelia rubbed her hand over the red material that was close to the center of the quilt. "Well, this is when I was reborn."

Grammy smiled. "I knew the day you brought that bloody shirt in here, something was burnin' in your belly."

"That day I met Bernard." She sighed, remembering the whole jumble of feelings from that day. Her mind had raced to find excuses for the dirt on her play dress. She didn't want to tell about being pushed to the ground. A bicycle fall always seemed a handy excuse. Sometimes she was sure Grammy had guessed the truth. And then there was her Superman, Bernard Howard.

Cordelia knew they were destined to marry from the moment she laid eyes on him and when she stole his cast-off shirt. "That day you started my quilt, too. I feel different now than when I was thirteen. How could that be a whole four years ago?"

Different wasn't exactly the right word. She still feared being deserted, and she was still very good at hiding her dirty secret about God. Older, yes. A more appropriate description.

She looked up. "Do you think someone my age could be in love?"

Grammy stroked Cordelia's hair. "Well, of course, child. In my day, girls close to your age were already married and birthing babies. You've got a good head on your shoulders. You know your own mind."

"Seems like only yesterday." Grammy continued as she rocked and cut squares. "Out of all the boys skulking around here at the time, why did you pick up with him?"

Cordelia knew all too vividly why Bernard had become her hero, but this was not the time to speak of her personal pain out loud. "Because I was worried over something he said that day about his father."

Grammy looked up from the pile of colored squares resting in her lap. "What did he say?"

"He said his father beat him." Those words made her hands shake after all these years.

Grammy Mae stopped rocking.

"And he said he was going to run away if he got beat again. I didn't understand why he would make such a big deal outta getting switched. Daddy always made me go out back to the willow tree and cut my own switch. That part was worse than getting hit, but I never thought of running away."

Although a switching usually consisted of more threat than action. She could only remember getting whacked a couple times. She'd learned that an instant performance of crying and screaming, regardless of how light the whack, would cause her father to relent.

Grammy Mae looked like a storm cloud was fixing to burst from her forehead. "I don't think the boy was talking about a regular switchin', baby. I think he could have been talking about a full-on man beatin'."

Cordelia nodded. "That's what I found out later. His father is a real nightmare. But he wouldn't try to beat him like that now because Bernard swears he'd fight back."

Grammy set her jaw.

Cordelia knew that look well. She needed to change topics before Grammy took off to Dix Court to punch Mr. Howard in the eye, or worse. "Tell me the story of my life covering again."

Cordelia glanced around the room at the piles of colored squares spread across the dressing table, ironing board, and bedspread. Over these past four years, the circular Pinecone Quilt pattern had grown to several feet in circumference.

Grammy's look softened. "Baby girl, I've told you the story of this quilt a dozen times. You should be able to recite it by heart."

"But I like to hear you say it." Actually, she enjoyed seeing the twinkle in Grammy's eyes as she talked.

Grammy Mae looked up, smiled, and then nodded her head. "I guessed it was up to me to teach you, since the tradition goes back as many generations as I can remember on our side of the family. This is a Pinecone Quilt. Some folks on my daddy's side of the family call it a Pine Burr Quilt, but it all works out to be the same pattern."

"You started working on it because Mom didn't like it."

"Now, Cordelia. Don't be startin' no trouble with your ma. I started your quilt because it was time someone got to work on it," said Grammy with a hint of annoyance in her voice. "It's not that she didn't like it. She didn't think it was necessary to give you a life covering."

Grammy and Ma were always at odds about the ways of the world. Ma called herself modern. Cordelia had caught her more than once mocking Grammy for talking about the olden days.

Her father told her their tussles resulted from two women, related only by marriage, of different generations, in the same house. Grammy was Daddy's mom. She liked to say she came from different stock than Ma's family. Sometimes Cordelia felt the tension between her ma and Grammy, but for the most part the two women stayed out of each other's way. Cordelia pretended not to pay much attention. But she adored Grammy, her confidant and ally.

Cordelia grinned. "She doesn't know how to quilt either."

"Baby girl, hush your mouth. The youngsters don't do a lot of the things we learned as girls. Now, let me tell the story."

Cordelia stifled a giggle at the thought of her mother navigating anything more complicated than the sales aisle at Woolworth's.

Grammy reached across and pulled folded muslin material into her lap, then shook it out across her knees. Concentric circles spaced about an inch and a half apart spread from the edge of the large completed circle.

"Our family tradition holds that the quiltmaker prays over each square, folding prayers into the triangles." Grammy grabbed up a square. She folded it diagonally to form a triangle; then, folding each outside point in, she created a square.

She held out the piece of green gingham material. "See this? I just folded in a prayer for your good health as I made the corners."

Cordelia fingered the square and glanced across the pile of cut pieces. "Where'd you get all this material?"

"From clothes that don't fit you anymore or special pieces of fabric I think you'll want to remember. They're your life moments, you know."

Grammy rocked softly as she measured and cut the squares with a large pair of sharp sewing shears. "Going back through the generations, each young lady is presented with her life covering on her eighteenth birthday. It holds the prayers, dreams, and wishes spoken for her and her life as a woman, wife, and mother. I was determined no granddaughter of mine was going to be without her own covering."

Cordelia fingered some of the squares. "Can I get yours out of the trunk?"

"Yes, baby, you may. I declare, as much as you fondle that old thing, you're going to rub all the colors off."

Cordelia lifted the lid of the steamer trunk at the foot of Grammy Mae's bed and sorted through several layers of clothing to find the quilt. The bold colors drew the usual gasp of pleasure from Cordelia. "Oh, Grammy, every time I look at this I think it gets more beautiful! Are you sure I couldn't have yours?"

"No, baby, every girl gets her own special quilt. These are the blessings for my life. You'll get your own blessings. I explained to you about Elijah and Elisha. Each had his own mantle. This one is yours." Grammy touched the quilt she was making. "You take care of your quilt, and it will take care of you."

"But your colors are quite beautiful."

"My quilt is made from clothes I wore when I was a youngster. Yours will have colors and prayers special just for you. It will be ready when you're eighteen."

Cordelia lifted her head to look at Grammy. "It seems like forever to get to eighteen."

Grammy Mae leaned her head back and laughed. "It's only a year away."

2

Bernard threw a handful of rabbit food into each hutch along the backyard fence. He didn't understand the waste of time feeding them when his father planned to butcher them in a day or two. Several years before, he'd chosen a rabbit as a pet. One day, to his horror, Butch was on the dinner menu. His father taunted him with the pelt. Now he avoided looking at the animals. It kept him from getting attached.

He stuffed the sad memory away as he slid the last door shut and leaned against the hutch. He wanted to think about his love . . . Cordelia Grace.

"Are you coming in here, Son?" His mother stood in the open doorway of the kitchen. "Your daddy'll be here any minute now. You know how he gets if you're not sitting at the table."

Bernard trudged across the yard, dropped the feedbag in the dust, vaulted up the back steps two at a time, and burst into the kitchen. His mother stood at the stove making his favorite dinner of pork chops and fried potatoes. The aroma made his stomach growl.

Her back to him, she flipped potatoes and poked at the sizzling pork chops.

"Mom, you're the best," he said as he wrapped his arms around her waist and hugged her. "That smells good!"

She playfully swatted him away. "You're going to squeeze the life out of me, Son. All this love is just because I'm filling your belly with good eats."

Bernard plopped onto a seat and spread his arms out onto the table. As he watched, Mom tipped her head and smiled at him. Nah. Really? No wonder Cordelia had felt familiar when he first met her. Her big brown eyes lit up like Mom's did when she smiled. And she tipped her head the same way too.

The kitchen door banged open, and Bernard tensed. He shoved his legs under the table, sat up straight, and took his elbows off the surface.

"Why isn't my dinner ready, woman?"

Mom's whole body tightened like a turtle tucking its head and legs into its shell.

Bernard held his breath.

"I'm setting your place now, Charles." She grabbed the stack of plates and silverware from the counter. Her hands shook, but the vinyl tablecloth muted any rattling sounds of plates and silverware. Mom had used a tablecloth ever since his father backhanded her when Bernard threw his plate at him. In reality, the plate had only slid an inch or so on the Formica top.

Bernard frowned.

"What's the matter with you, boy?" Charles took the seat at the head of the table. "Did you go down to the coal breaker today and pick enough coal for the stove?"

"Yes, when I got out of work, I went." Bernard erased the frown, but the muscles at the back of his neck tightened, and he answered with a hint of defiance. At the age of seventeen, he hated being called boy. But it was safer to suffer in silence than cause a fuss.

Charles glared at him. "Yes, what?"

Bernard averted his eyes. "Yes, *sir*, I went and got coal."

Anna hurried the dish of potatoes into the center of the table and returned with the platter of three large pork chops. She slid into her seat opposite Bernard and forked a pork chop onto Charles's plate and one onto Bernard's.

"Is this all I get? One lousy pork chop? I work in the mines all day to support this family, and all I get to eat is barely enough to keep a bird alive," barked Charles. "What do you do with all my money, you ungrateful woman? Are you buying more things for this boy? It's a good thing there's only one of them to be sucking me dry."

Anna showed no emotion as she forked the last pork chop onto his plate.

Bernard pulled his eyebrows together and lowered his head enough to show his displeasure. She gave an almost imperceptible shake of her head, then scooped an extra large helping of fried potatoes onto her own empty plate.

Charles was too busy peppering his food to notice the exchange. He reached for the salt and shook it over the meat. Nothing came out. He shook it again. Still nothing. "Woman, what have I told you about giving me an empty saltshaker?"

Anna registered shock. "I'm sorry. I washed it this afternoon and let it dry. I must have screwed the lid on without paying attention." She plucked the shaker from his hand and scurried to the cupboard. She returned in a moment with the filled saltshaker. Anna's hand trembled as she set it on the table and took her seat.

Charles lifted his hand and accidentally brushed the shaker off the table. The porcelain shaker broke into several pieces and salt spread across the linoleum floor.

"Look what you've done, you stupid woman!" Charles backhanded Anna, knocking her off her chair.

Bernard scrambled around the table to his mother. "Ma, are you all right?"

He reached to help her rise, putting himself between her and his father. He didn't want her hit again.

"I'm all right, Son, I just slipped," His mother's face flushed as she tried to climb back into her chair.

Bernard could see that she was dizzy. "You didn't slip! He hit you." He searched her eyes for any glimmer of defiance and hoped that she would balk at his father's bad behavior.

She gently put her trembling fingers to his lips.

He shook her hand away.

"What did you say?" snarled Charles. "Are you calling your mother a liar?"

Bernard spun to face him. "I saw you hit her."

Charles pointed his fork at him. "You need to learn to keep quiet in *my* house, boy."

"Everybody knows you hit her. I don't understand why she keeps protecting you."

Charles bolted upright. His chair tipped over, slamming to the floor. "What goes on in this house stays in this house!"

"Why? So you can continue to use her as a punching bag—"

Charles's fist thrust forward.

Bernard blocked the punch and grabbed him by the wrist.

Charles glared. "Let go of my arm."

Bernard stared him down. "I've told you before. I'm not a child anymore, and you will not hit me without consequences."

Charles swore under his breath and jerked his hand back from Bernard's grasp. He turned away. Then spun back and rammed the heels of both hands into Bernard's chest.

Anna whimpered.

Bernard stumbled back, lost his balance, and crashed onto the floor at the base of the refrigerator. He smacked the side of his face against the metal.

He raised the back of his hand to his lips. A smear of blood ran from knuckle to wrist. Hatred pounded through his heart as his eyes rose to glare at his father. The man wasn't paying him any attention. He had gone back to eating. Bernard saw the stricken look in his mother's face. His anger subsided for her sake. Eight months until he could be free. His mother refused to give her blessing for him to move out before then, and he loved her too much to defy her. He feared leaving his mother with this animal, but he couldn't save her and himself.

On January 15, 1943, Bernard would celebrate his eighteenth birthday and his freedom.

3

Cordelia sat in her favorite spot on the waist-high wall that surrounded Scranton Technical High School. The flat stone emanated the day's sunshine. The warmth relaxed her while she waited. Her girlfriends always met near the front doors after school on Wednesdays.

She stole a few glances at her new dress designs while she waited for the crew. How could she make beautiful clothes when Bernard felt a woman belonged at home and should raise the children? To her distress, her father and Bernard actually agreed about this.

"What's cookin', baby doll?"

Cordelia flinched. Her eyes widened as her fingers clutched the pages, wrinkling the paper. She lifted her head in the speaker's direction. "Marcie Ballenger! You scared the snot right out of me!" She blew out a huff of air and patted her chest. "Making your voice low like that, I thought for a second you were Bernard."

Marcie snorted with laughter. "Jeepers creepers, I didn't know you were worried about him seeing your sketches."

"I'm not." Cordelia averted her eyes. "Who needs the male ego?" Talking about a job always caused an argument.

"Wait a minute. I don't like the way you said that." She stepped in closer. "Is he intimidating you some other way?"

Cordelia's eyes grew wide. "No, never! Bernard would never hurt me. I just don't want to disappoint him. He wondered if I wanted a job because I was afraid that he couldn't take care of me like a husband should."

"Boy oh boy, men are completely insecure," laughed Marcie.

"Not insecure, but he said it made him feel incompetent." She stuffed her dreams away because Bernard meant everything in the world to her. He was her Superman.

One close call for the day was enough. She smoothed and put the pages back in order, deciding not to press her luck as she shoved them back into her book bag. *Luck.* Grammy hated those four letters. She corrected Cordelia often. There was only God, and no such thing as luck.

She would have to remember to thank God when she worked on the quilt with Grammy. She had avoided another opportunity to hurt Bernard's feelings with her fanciful dreams. Maybe she could ask Grammy to add a prayer into her quilt for a job. But that meant she'd have to buy into the quilt as a mantle on her life. Did she believe in the quilt? Or was she just working on it to please Grammy?

"Are you going to talk to me?" Marcie hopped onto the wall next to Cordelia. She swung her legs. Her scuffed saddle shoes grated against the rough soapstone.

Cordelia snapped out of her thoughts and smiled. "Of course I'm talking to you. You're my best friend." She turned to look at Marcie. "Do you have a quilt?"

"A quilt? What kind of quilt?"

"A Pinecone Quilt. My Grammy's making one for my eighteenth birthday."

"No, I don't have one, but I have a cousin who does. My Gram died before I was born. My mom's a dynamite cook, but she can't sew a button on, let alone make something like that."

Cordelia smiled. "My mom can't sew either."

"Why do you want to know?"

"Grammy is putting a lot of effort into it and praying over each piece. Is she just old, or is that normal?" Cordelia's mom had been making random snide remarks at the dinner table lately. The two women seemed ready for all-out war over this quilt. Meanwhile, Dad ate in silence and kept his head down.

Marcie laughed. "Well, praying is always normal. You surprise me."

"Why? Because I wonder if prayer works?"

"Yeah, I expect a preacher's kid to pray about everything, including your grades."

Cordelia smiled. "Or at least about Bernard warming to the notion of me getting a job." Maybe prayer would make him change his mind. It was worth a try. Sometimes it all confused her. Listening to and watching adults made her question everything she'd been taught about God.

"Are you worried about him seeing your designs?" Marcie again whacked the wall with her shoes.

Cordelia nodded. "Designing clothes is my dream job. I really want to do that more than anything. Well . . . not more than marrying Bernard. But is it a bad thing that I want a job?"

"Girl, he's got more stubbornness in him than two mules. You'd better find a new man, because his mind is set." Marcie was a real warrior when it came to being her own person. She did not let a man tell her what to do.

"Well, what more could I want? Bernard is my future. I've loved him since I was—"

"Yeah, I know," Marcie clutched her chest in feigned emotion. "You've loved him since you were thirteen. That and five cents will get you a Royal Crown Cola."

Cordelia glared at her. She could feel her cheeks getting warm. "That's not fair. Bernard is a good guy, and he loves me. He just wants his wife to stay at home. Even though I'd rather drink castor oil three times a day than be a housewife."

Marcie wagged her head from side to side. "I know. I'm just pulling your leg. My dad is the same way about women having jobs." She turned to face Cordelia. "You know something? My mom talked to some of her lady friends. They were saying that 'cause of this war stuff, more women are going to work." She bent close and said, almost whispering, "My own mom is talking about getting a position at Scranton Button."

"No! Hot diggity." Cordelia slapped her hand onto Marcie's knee. "What did your dad say?"

"I think he's actually going to let her do it. With all these ads about patriotism, it looks like he's changing his mind."

"You really think so?" Cordelia felt a flutter of excitement.

"Yep. Dad said with all the young men getting drafted to war, women are the only ones left to fill all those empty spots in the factories. Mom said the shirt factory down in Kressler Court is going to start making army uniforms next month. They need a lot of women to sew. They're passing out applications."

Cordelia clapped her hands and hopped off the wall. "That means most all the neighborhood women will be getting jobs. Maybe I'll have a chance of getting a summer job."

"Not if I have anything to say about it," said Bernard.

Cordelia glanced right, and then left. All she could see was his black fedora bobbing along the edge of the stone wall. First the top of his head, then those stunning green eyes came into view as he peered over the wall. He strolled around the corner and over to the girls.

Cordelia's heart always pounded harder when she saw Bernard. A job at Stoney's Garage gave his seventeen-year-old body more muscle than most grown men could muster. He was swoon-worthy handsome.

He gathered her into his arms. She rested her head on his muscular chest the way she had seen the heroines do in motion pictures. She blushed at the prickles of arousal growing inside her. That kind of behavior would have to wait until they married, which was a year away yet. But the tingle sure made her want to hurry the process all the more.

Ignoring her subconscious, she wanted to be angry with him. She pushed away and glanced first at her book bag to be sure her designs weren't showing. "Don't go blowing any fuses. We weren't the ones talking. It was our parents." She clenched her fists and planted them firmly on her hips.

Bernard leaned back against the wall next to Marcie, slid his left hand into his trouser pocket, and rested his right elbow on the stone wall. His arm muscles bulged in the tight-fitting T-shirt. "Why were your parents talking about women working?"

"Because of the war, silly." Marcie squinted with one eye. "Aren't you old enough to get drafted yet?"

"Marcie!" Cordelia whacked her friend's arm. "No, he's not old enough yet, and this war is going to be over before he has to sign up. We're getting married next year."

Her chest clutched. Thinking of Bernard leaving her, or in harm's way, stole her breath.

Bernard stared at both of them, apparently unfazed by thoughts of war. "Are one of you going to answer me?"

"About what?" Cordelia tipped her head to the side. Maybe if she flirted, it would distract him.

"Don't play dumb, doll face . . . about the women working."

Cordelia fidgeted with her hands, avoiding eye contact with him. She didn't want to lie.

Marcie broke the tension by changing the subject. "Hey, are you two coming to the paper bag party on Friday night? It's going to be a real hoot."

Those stupid segregated parties set Cordelia's teeth on edge. She was usually clever enough to avoid them without offending her friends. But today she appreciated the distracting thought. She knew it would be an effective change of subject. "It sounds like a great—"

"Cordelia, no!" Bernard wheeled to Marcie. "That's just plain mean. It's bad enough other folks treat Negroes as second class, but for Negroes to be treating each other that way is just plain wrong." He grabbed for Cordelia's hand and headed toward the corner with her in tow.

Cordelia grimaced at Marcie and snatched her book bag, not that she had much of a choice about going with him, considering the grip he had on her hand. She hurried to keep in step with his long strides.

"Bernard, what's wrong with you? Why are you angry?" Cordelia tried to tug her hand free, but he didn't release his grip. They had walked down the hill to the end of the high school and turned into Dix Court before he relaxed.

He turned to face her. "Do you really think it's fun to go to a party that excludes people darker than a paper bag?"

Cordelia's face grew warm. She didn't particularly like the idea either, but since he was extremely bossy about it, she countered, "Well . . . these are our friends. It's a polite way of excluding the people we don't hang around."

Bernard shook his head as though trying to keep the thought from sticking to his brain. "Polite! Listen to yourself! You and your friends are not hanging around with other Negro kids because they are too dark for you. That's about as stuck-up and snotty as I've ever heard." He stormed down the alley.

Her eyes flashed with anger, but she ran to keep pace with his stride. "Are you calling me stuck-up and snotty?" Her lips pursed tighter than the knot in her shoe.

Bernard skidded to a halt. "You'd better ask God what you sound like talking that way."

"Ask God?" This conversation was going downhill fast. "There you go sounding just like my father. I'm tired of you two putting everything on God."

Every answer her father gave her ended with an admonishment to talk to God. After watching her parents' behavior, followed by church on Sunday all pious-like, she noticed that they hadn't spent *any* time asking God for *any*thing. Her father always said, "Do as I say, not as I do." Seventeen didn't mean she was blind and stupid.

"Your father is our pastor. What would you expect him to tell you to do, go ask your girlfriends?" Bernard touched her arm. "Don't you have any compassion for kids worse off than us?"

She shook off his hand. "What's wrong with you today?"

Bernard walked to the end of the alley in silence, crossed Pine Street, and continued up Dix Court toward his house.

"Bernard?" Cordelia hurried to catch up to him. "I asked you what's wrong?"

He stopped.

She searched his eyes for a hint of emotion. The flecks of gray in his green eyes seemed to refract the light. They glistened. Or maybe it was the moisture accumulating in the corners. She didn't understand or even want to think that he looked like he was about to cry.

"You're scaring me."

"Akira Hirabayashi and his family are gone."

"Gone?" Cordelia stared at him. "Where did they go? When are they coming back? Who's going to run the nursery? Mom said this morning she was going to put in her flower garden orders."

"The FBI took the whole family away because Mr. Hirabayashi's brother came from California to avoid an internment camp."

"Why would they try to put them in an internment camp?"

"They thought the whole family could be a threat. The G-men weren't very nice. They only let each person take one suitcase." He let the news sink in. "Mr. Moore, their next-door neighbor, said he would watch the house and nursery while they were gone. Mr. Hirabayashi asked the G-man when they'd be back. They told him they didn't know."

"There must be some mistake."

"There's no mistake." Bernard shook his head. "My father said they were taken away because the government thinks the Japanese living in this country could be sympathizers with the Japanese that bombed Pearl Harbor."

"But Akira was born here in Scranton. His family's lived here forever. They're good people."

"Good . . . but different. Like I've been trying to make you understand about the kids not invited to that stupid party."

Cordelia stiffened. She wanted to agree. But not when he acted so pious. "Oh, that's why you told me about the Hirabayashis. You wanted to dig at me again about the party." She strode off, past Bernard's house, past Stoney's, to the end of the alley.

4

All the way down Olive Street, she argued with an invisible Bernard. She passed two old ladies walking along the street arm in arm. They chattered like magpies but stopped as she passed. She glanced back. They turned and watched her own animated conversation as she tromped down the hill to the Avenue. It didn't stop her. *Men!*

She was still muttering under her breath as the screen door slammed behind her. But the storm cloud lifted as she charged into the living room. The house was wonderfully cool compared to the heat outside, and to what simmered in her brain. She stopped. Angry voices came from the back of the house. Cordelia tiptoed into the dining room to listen. She knew it wasn't polite to eavesdrop, but she knew those voices. Mom and Grammy . . . again.

"You've been making that quilt since she was thirteen. I'm beginning to think you're using it as a way of getting her attention, to make me look bad," said Mom.

"Don't be ridiculous, Betty. This is not a personal affront to you. Making a quilt for Cordelia is something I've planned since she was born. Why would it make you look bad?"

Grammy spoke in an even tone. Cordelia could picture her rocking as she talked.

"Because no one in my family ever quilted. It makes us seem incapable. Besides, you're filling her head with nonsense about it being a prayer covering for her life." Mom's voice rose the way it did when she argued with Cordelia and was losing ground in the debate.

Grammy countered, "I'm sorry your family doesn't quilt as a tradition, but you've never been motivated to try it either. There is nothing wrong with praying for my granddaughter and giving her a physical reminder that I did."

"You're creating a false sense of security that all your prayers for her life will be answered," said Mom.

"What is wrong with you? I've never known a professing Christian to be quite this opposed to prayer. How do you know they won't be answered?"

"Because God only helps those who help themselves."

"That saying is an old wives' tale. It's not in the Bible, and it's a lie straight from the enemy's pit," charged Gram.

"You are way behind the times. All you need to do is see your success in your mind and claim it."

"You and that Board have gone and led my son into preaching that health and money gospel. That stuff fills the pews, but it lacks any talk about sin. Rich and happy does not show the way. Believe me, I pray for your souls every day," answered Grammy.

They were getting deep. If they caught her listening, Grammy and Mom would both be mad. She turned to leave.

"Waste your time if you want to. Going to the store and buying her a blanket would be cheaper and take less time and effort," yelled Mom.

Grammy's door closed hard.

Cordelia hightailed it out of the house, then scrambled down the porch steps and into the yard. How long should she wait before going back in? She stared at the front door. Was her mom right? Was it nonsense to pray?

The distraction almost made her forget her anger at Bernard. But now it bubbled back to the surface. She mounted the steps and slammed the front door to be sure she could be heard.

Betty Grace sat on the overstuffed couch across from the floor model radio. She was an elegant figure, the perfect home-maker, and First Lady of the church. She wore the requisite strand of pearls around her slender throat, and single pearl earrings peeked from beneath her meticulous finger-waved curls. Her pink dress and matching high heels made her light caramel skin look delicate against the dark blue brocade couch as she crocheted along the edges of a white handkerchief.

Mom's soft laughter at the radio characters' banter soothed Cordelia's rattled mood. Maybe Mom was right. It might be easier to just think positive thoughts and not have to invest all that time in prayer.

She plopped onto the couch next to her mom. "Why are boys such a pain in the neck?" First things first. Besides, she didn't want to let on that she'd heard their argument.

Betty smiled and turned the radio volume down a touch. As she leaned back, she wrapped an arm around Cordelia's shoulder as though nothing bad had transpired.

"Are we talking about boys in general or one boy in particular?" Her tone was now as soft as her appearance.

Cordelia didn't want to revisit the paper bag party discussion with her mother. "One boy in particular."

Betty smiled and went back to crocheting. "What has Bernard done now? I've told you many times, my sweet, men don't think the same way women do."

Cordelia needed to pick her battles. She pulled the sketches out of her book bag and laid them on her mom's lap.

Betty winked. "Ah, this conversation is about you getting a job again."

She decided to ignore that remark. Her mother loved nice clothes. "What do you think? I designed these using those new zippers that are all the rage. They're much less expensive than buttons. I know there's not a lot of material available now, but soon as this war's over there'll be plenty to go around. My teacher thinks that I'm really good and could get a job at a dressmaking shop." She spun the words like a spool of thread, fearful if she paused, her mother might cut her off.

"Yes, and with more women having jobs because of the war, they'll have more money to spend on fine clothes later on." Betty handled each sketch in turn. "These designs are beautiful. I love the different hemlines."

Cordelia forgot her anger toward Bernard. This was the perfect time to talk about a job.

"Different hemlines are going to be all the latest fad, Mom. Mid-calf for day and long for evening. And I really want to create new styles for ladies." She hoped that the look on her face pleaded with her mom for agreement.

The radio show ended and strains of Duke Ellington's "It Don't Mean a Thing if It Ain't Got That Swing," drifted out of the polished mahogany radio.

Betty laughed. "The course of this conversation is about getting a job when you finish school next year."

"Could I, please?" Cordelia smiled at her mom. "My teacher said I'm a really good seamstress. She has a lady friend who owns a dress shop who would be glad to give me a job."

Betty leaned her head on the high back of the couch. She glanced to the ceiling and rested her hands in her lap. "Ah, and therein lies the conundrum. Your father and Bernard are both against you working."

"But you're not against it."

Betty leaned forward. "No, I'm not. I think you should be able to do what you wish as long as it's honorable. But your father and Bernard are men. Not only are men the head of the family, but it threatens their masculinity if they can't provide for their families."

Cordelia looked at her mother from a fresh perspective. "Is that why you don't work, Mom?"

Betty smiled and shook her head. "No, my sweet. You need to learn how to approach a subject with a husband when you truly want something. Your father couldn't stop me if I put my mind to it. I don't work because I don't choose to. You have to realize a job is not a new thing to Negro women. Many of the women in this town work, whether it's in someone's house or in one of the sewing factories."

"Most of my friends' mothers don't work."

"That's because their fathers have good enough jobs or their sons are pressed to work . . . like your Bernard."

Cordelia grimaced. "Bernard didn't want to quit school at sixteen. His father said that if he didn't, Bernard's mother would have to clean houses. That broke Bernard's heart. He went to work for Stoney Hansen."

"He's going to make a right fine man, that boy. You watch how a man treats his momma and you know how he'll treat you." Betty patted her on the shoulder and rose from the couch. "I have to get dinner started. Your father will be home from the church any time now. He wants to catch the Dodgers game on the radio this evening."

Cordelia nodded and gathered her pages. Maybe Grammy would be more sympathetic to her cause. Strains of the Andrews Sisters' "Boogie Woogie Bugle Boy" followed her out of the living room as she scooted through the kitchen to Grammy's room.

The door stood ajar. Grammy Mae rocked and stitched in serenity on the Pinecone Quilt. The disagreement didn't seem to have affected her mood. Her lips moved, forming silent words as she folded each small square of fabric. First she made a triangle, then she folded down each outer point to form a square envelope, and then she sewed the piece into place. She repeated the process again and again. The glow around Grammy was almost visible, tangible to Cordelia, like she could reach out and touch it to gain Grammy's peace and wisdom. She admired Grammy's relationship with God, though she didn't understand how to have one herself. Many different adult opinions confused her.

She tapped on the door, not wanting to break the magic. Grammy Mae lifted her glance and motioned. A smile spread across her aged face.

"And how was school today, baby girl?"

Cordelia sat on the edge of the bed closest to the rocker. "Oh, Grammy, I'm not a baby girl." She looked at Grammy closely. Not a hint of the argument.

"Well, no matter your age, to me you'll always be my baby girl." She chuckled. "What seems to be botherin' your grown self today?"

Cordelia shuffled her feet on the circular rag rug in front of the bed. She couldn't fool Grammy when she had a problem. "I'm mad at Bernard."

"What'd that sweet boy do now?"

"Nothing." She heaved an exaggerated sigh.

Grammy Mae chuckled again. "Seems to me there's a whole lot of sighin' goin' on for *nothing*."

"He made me defend something I didn't even want to defend. He demanded I agree with him and I didn't want to let him think he could tell me what to do."

Grammy Mae stopped rocking. Her shoulders convulsed in silent laughter, and she shook her head. "Would you like to translate for an old lady?"

The words poured out in a flood of emotion. "I didn't even want to go to the stupid paper bag party. Before I had a chance to say no, he demanded I not go. Then I had to defend it because I wasn't letting him tell me what to do, especially not in front of my friend." Her brow furrowed, and she kicked at the rug. She had to put the kibosh on that fast before Marcie nagged her about it forever.

"Oh, I see. They still have those kinds of parties, do they?"

Cordelia felt the heat rise in her face. "Yes, ma'am," she lowered her gaze.

"That's as bad as segregation, exceptin' it's Negroes doin' it to their own kind just 'cause they're darker. You understand that's very mean, don't you?"

"Yes, ma'am." In reality, she'd survived her childhood by sticking with the light-complexioned kids. They were picked on the same as her, but it was a safety in numbers thing.

"Lord knows, I prayed for your childhood, for your protection from the mean ones that called you *high yella*."

Cordelia's glance lifted and looked directly at Grammy Mae. "You knew?"

"Of course, child, in case you haven't noticed, our whole family going back two generations is mulatto. We've all been through the same meanness as you young'uns."

"I spent a lot of time feeling alone."

"I heard the taunts sometimes out in the backyard. Sound travels from that alley right well. I prayed for you real hard, and the Lord sent other families . . . and he sent Bernard." She reached over and patted Cordelia's hand.

"You prayed for me?"

"Yes, baby, I've always prayed for you. On a daily basis, especially about your friends."

"Well, now I'm older, I have friends I'm comfortable with, and I can't help it that they're all light."

"Have you ever tried to befriend any of the other children?"

Cordelia bit down hard on her lip. She tasted blood and remembered the blood some of those fights had drawn. "No, ma'am. We never have anything in common."

"You mean because they are darker?"

"It's easier to keep my distance."

"Do you remember the Wilson kids?"

A shiver of memory crept along her back and out of her shoulder, making her head shudder. "I remember I was glad when they moved away."

"Did you know those kids didn't have a momma?"

Cordelia suddenly felt small. "No, I didn't. What happened to her?"

"Mrs. Wilson died in childbirth, and her husband took to the bottle to console himself. Those children ran pretty much wild until Children's Aid came and took them all away the year you turned fourteen."

"That's why they moved? I never knew."

"You weren't told because some hardship ain't for children to bear. But Lord knows, everybody has a story, and a hardship. We all have to learn to look through the meanness to their pain."

"How, when every part of you says run away from them?"

"You have to learn to trust in the Lord when times are hard. We can't always see where the Lord is leadin' us. His ways are not our ways. If we understood where He was taking us, then we wouldn't need faith and we wouldn't need to pray, now would we?"

"No, I guess not." Cordelia needed to think and probably talk to more of her friends to see what they thought about praying. She couldn't remember the subject ever coming up, especially outside of church.

Grammy smiled and stitched another piece into place. "See this section here?" She spread her hand across two circular rows of pale yellow material. "This is the dress you wore to church the first time you sang "Yes, Jesus Loves Me" as a five-year-old. You had innocent, childlike faith."

Cordelia touched the material. "Do you save everything?"

"Just the milestones. Your awakening to faith was important to me. You used to look quite cute kneeling beside your bed at night with your little hands folded in prayer."

Cordelia did a fast mental rewind. She had prayed for everything, including her dolls and the neighbor's dog. What had happened to those days?

Cordelia knelt on the floor and put her head in Grammy Mae's lap. When she was thirty years old, she'd still put her head in her grandmother's lap, where she felt safe and loved. "I don't know why I stopped. My daddy's the preacher and I don't understand the Lord like you do. Sometimes I don't know if I want to."

Grammy Mae stroked her hair, soothing her heart. "Why do you say that, baby?"

"Because adults are hypocritical. I see them at church acting all prim and proper. Then they go home and act like the devil for the rest of the week." They sure weren't spending their time in prayer. Now she had second thoughts about asking for a prayer to get a job. Maybe she should do what her mom had suggested, just declare she wanted a job and wait for it to show.

Grammy chuckled. "That's the way of the world we live in, child. But it's on each of us to make our own way with the Lord."

Cordelia shook her head. "Maybe when I'm your age. I don't think I want to right now."

"Of course you want to. No grandchild of mine is going to walk around without a Jesus relationship. That's why we've spent these past few years working on your quilt and me teaching you about prayer. It'll come to you when you need it. Some of us just have a little harder time with the learnin' part than others."

Cordelia looked at her and squeezed her eyes shut. *Oh, Lord.* And she didn't mean it as a prayer. She felt like a fraud. How long could this go on? Was God going to smack her with a lightning bolt or something for not having enough faith to pray?

5

Bernard watched Cordelia run down the alley without trying to stop her. Truth be told, he didn't know *what* to say. He didn't understand why girls saw all these petty differences in each other. Guys got along, all shades of color and ethnic background being equal, and if they didn't, they fought and moved past it. His father, in one of his nicer moments, said there's no understanding women. Bernard took solace in at least one point where he agreed with his father.

He finished cleaning cages and feeding rabbits while carrying on an internal conversation with God. The old people at church talked about going into a quiet room with their Bibles to meditate. Bernard's best communication with the Lord happened while he worked with the animals. Maybe being outside under the sun and sky, or at night under the stars, brought him closer to the Lord.

He sat on the steps and looked at the late afternoon sky. "Lord, I really could use some help in understanding women." But this conversation wasn't getting him anywhere. He thought he heard the Lord laugh at him.

He kicked at a pebble in the dust and folded his hands together, resting his elbows on his spread knees. "She wants to get a job, Lord." He shook his head. "I'm supposed to be the man of my household. Shouldn't I be the one taking care of her, not the other way around? Doesn't she trust me to take care of her?"

Still no answer. Maybe he was asking the wrong questions, or maybe his frame of mind stopped him from hearing the Lord's answers.

The screen door behind him squeaked open. "Bernard, why are you still out here? I thought with your father working an extra shift in the mines, you'd be in the living room playing records on the Victrola. You don't get a lot of chances to listen to your music."

Bernard shook his head. "I know, Ma. I was talking to God."

Anna looked around and then at the sky as though searching for someone. "Did he answer you back?"

Bernard loved his mother dearly, but neither she nor his father had much time for the church other than Christmas or Easter Sunday. His father often joked that if he went any more often the roof might cave in. Bernard knew better than to chastise his father for irreverence against the Lord, but his mother seemed to have a wall up that Bernard didn't know how to break through.

He rose and dusted himself off. "No, Ma, he didn't answer me back . . . this time. But he will. The Lord is faithful that way."

—∞—

Anna tried to give a noncommittal look. Bernard smiled and kissed her on the forehead as he passed by. She heard him bound up the stairs and then back down. It didn't take but five minutes before the sounds of Louis Armstrong's "On the Sunny Side of the Street" drifted through the house. Her feet tapped out the beat as she peeled potatoes and shucked the corn for their dinner. She almost didn't hear the soft rap on the door.

Anna wiped her hands on her apron. She parted the curtain on the crosshatched door window. Her heartbeat ramped up. Reverend Emanuel Grace stood on the other side. She fumbled to open the door for the preacher. With shaking fingers, she pushed the stray hairs behind her ears.

"Reverend Grace, well, I declare, I wasn't expecting to see you. I must look a fright." She directed her gaze to the floor.

"Hello, Mrs. Howard. I must say that I've been expecting to see you at church sooner rather than later." He smiled as though he delivered that same message quite often. "You know, we're open every Sunday, regular as clockwork."

She shifted her weight from foot to foot. "What can I do for you, Reverend?"

"May I come in?"

Anna backed away from the open door. "Of course; I'm sorry for being rude."

Reverend Grace entered and removed his fedora. His hair, prematurely graying at the temples, was slicked back smooth and shiny with Murray's pomade. Anna could tell the difference between the waxy smell of NuNile, the lavender of Royal Crown, and the coconut oil of Murray's.

"I would like to talk to Bernard, if that's possible."

Anna released the breath she held. She wouldn't be subjected to a sermon today, and her husband wasn't home to act badly at the unannounced intrusion. Bernard respected the man, or she wouldn't have let him in at all. "He's in the living room, Reverend. This way, please."

Bernard stood in front of the Victrola. His head bobbed as he sorted through his record albums.

"Son, may I have a word with you?"

Bernard spun on his heels. Reverend Grace stood with his hat in hand, smiling.

"Pastor, come in. Sit down." He motioned to the heavy wing-backed chairs on each side of the lamp table. He lifted the needle from the record, and the room fell silent.

Bernard eased into the other chair, pleased to have a visit from the Reverend. A niggle of guilt threaded through his gut. He looked more to the pastor for guidance than to his own father, but his father didn't want to talk about God.

"What brings you back into the Court this time of day?" Bernard smiled. "I know your Dodgers are playing St. Louis tonight and the game will be on the radio." He chuckled. "I still haven't gotten over the Dodgers beating the Phillies last year." In one of his father's rare good moods, he'd taken him to Shibe Park in North Philadelphia for that game. There were two reasons for Bernard to remember it.

Reverend Grace smiled. "Yes, I remember, and they're doing well again this year. They've won the last eight games. I don't want to miss it."

Bernard laughed. He and the reverend had a friendly rivalry. But when the Philadelphia Stars played, they banded together to root for the Negro League team.

Reverend Grace grew serious. "I wanted to talk to you about our young people at church. I think you'd make a fine assistant leader, and with summer coming, we need the help."

Bernard felt a rush of pride that Reverend Grace would think highly of him. He could see his mother's shadow in the kitchen doorway. She had stayed out of sight but within earshot. "I . . . I don't know what to say, Pastor. I'm honored.

Are you sure this is something I should do? There are other capable guys in our group."

Reverend Grace laid his hat on the arm of the couch across from them. "I'm glad to see you acknowledge others, but my daughter is deeply taken with you, and believe me, I've watched your behavior with her—"

Bernard felt a warmth rising in his face. "Sir, I have nothing but the highest respect for your daughter." Could he bring the words out in front of his pastor? His hands turned clammy. "I love her," his head dipped slightly, "and I want to ask you for her hand in marriage next year—"

"Like I said, I've watched you. I believe your intentions are honorable." The reverend nodded and a half smile creased his face as he leaned forward. "I think of you as the son I never had. I've watched you grow into a fine young man. Your Bible studies and love for the Lord convinced me you're the right young man for the job."

Bernard was excited and dismayed all at the same time. Handed a great honor, but having no one to share the excitement with other than Cordelia. His parents didn't understand his true affection for God and the church.

He rubbed his hands together in anticipation. "I'll work really hard to do the best I can. I won't let you down."

Reverend Grace stood. "I know, Bernard. You've overcome great odds to get where you are today."

Bernard stood and shook his hand. All he saw from the corner of his eye was the flash of his mother's tan housedress as she stormed into the room to face the reverend.

"What do you mean by *he's overcome great odds*?" Anna's right hand was balled up into a knot on her hip, while her left hand snapped a dish towel in the air. "Are you trying to say my boy is dumb or something?"

"Ma!" Bernard tried to hush her, but she lifted the dish towel and silenced him.

Reverend Grace cut in. "I meant his studies are self-directed."

"I think you're saying me and my husband are the stupid ones." Anna's nostrils flared.

"I meant that neither you nor your husband are involved in the church. Usually children left to their own devices aren't as grounded in Scripture as Bernard is."

"Oh, now you're calling us heathens. Is that it? Well, let me tell you, Bernard was raised in the church until he was twelve. Me and my husband were part of a church. A big church!"

"I assure you I meant no disrespect." Reverend Grace looked first at Bernard and then at Anna. "Your son has a gift that should be shared with other young people to encourage their walk with the Lord."

"Oh, is that right? And what happens when he displeases you? Or, heaven forbid, he slips off the pedestal you're putting him on, and he sins. I know. Then you'll push him aside like garbage."

"Mrs. Howard, no one will push Bernard away. We don't push anyone away for sinning. There are no perfect people. Only our Lord was perfect. I don't understand why you believe he would be abandoned."

"Because we were." Anna used the hand holding the dish towel to point toward the door. "That's right! You go on your way. You're just like they were, treatin' us like we're dirt. Like we're not good enough."

Tears puddled in her eyes and rolled down her cheeks. "It wasn't my fault."

Bernard's jaw went slack. He reached out to touch his mother but her shoulders convulsed. He drew back his hand and looked at the reverend, helpless.

"I'm sorry, Reverend. I don't know what's gotten into her."

"Gotten into me?" Her voice rose an octave. "I thought God was supposed to love us no matter what."

Bernard felt his face getting hot. Where did this tirade come from? "Ma, please, Pastor didn't—"

"I told you to shush, boy." Anna glared at him. "This is between me and the reverend here."

Reverend Grace spoke softly. "Mrs. Howard, you look like you want to talk. Would you like me to listen?"

"I done said enough. I don't want you hurtin' my boy, that's all. Been enough pain from God and judgment and sin."

"No one is going to hurt your boy. You heard me say I think of him like the son I never had. I only want the best for him."

Anna suddenly deflated, sinking to her knees as if the invisible weight on her shoulders was more than she could bear. "I want more than the best for him. Always did. Tried to do right by him. Always tried to do right." She lifted her head and a river of tears splashed onto the front of her housedress. "God judged me and I accept that, but I won't have him hurting my boy. God's too mean."

Reverend Grace laid his hat on the seat of the chair and went over to Anna. "Mrs. Howard, I don't know what pain you've been through, but God loves you no matter what. No sin is too great for God. Jesus died for all of our sins, past, present, and future."

"No, no-oo." She shook her head strongly, knocking herself off balance. "Carried this too long. Time it was said and done."

Bernard put his hand on her arm to help her up, but she shook him off and stood on her own. "It wasn't my fault." She gripped Bernard's shirt. "Your father made me do it. Almost bled to death, and all they could say was it was God's judgment on my sin."

Bernard looked at Reverend Grace.

Reverend Grace shook his head but turned to Anna. "Would you like to talk about it with me?"

Anna let her shoulders slump, then pulled back. "No! The church showed me just what they were made of, and I ain't going back for seconds."

"Ma, what is wrong? Let Reverend Grace help."

She spit the words out. "Reverend Grace can't help me now."

"You're scaring me. I never saw you this upset, not even when Dad—" He caught himself. What happened in the house stayed in the house.

"No one can help me now. I can't have no more children." She stared off into space. "Maybe that *was* a gift from God. Saved another child from having to live in this mess."

Reverend Grace looked helpless now, as though he weren't prepared for an impromptu confession.

"Ma, please. What's the matter?"

She mumbled.

Reverend Grace and Bernard looked at each other and then back at her.

"It's time I said it out loud." She buried her head in her hands. "I had an abortion."

Bernard stumbled back against the chair but caught himself before he fell. "Ma, what are you saying?"

She ran her hand through her hair as though to wipe the memory to the back of her head. "I got pregnant when you were twelve. Your father didn't want any more children. He made me get rid of the baby."

Bernard squeezed his eyes shut, like it would keep the picture from searing itself into his brain. His stomach lurched. He tasted bile as he brought his hand to his mouth.

Anna began to weep softly, rocking back and forth. Reverend Grace touched her arm. She yanked it away.

"It was a vile woman that lived in an alley that did it." Anna inched to the couch, as though she feared her legs wouldn't make it that far.

She turned to face the two stunned men. "She made me lay on a filthy, smelly cot. There were blood stains on the sheets. I protested. I changed my mind and tried to leave, but she wouldn't give me the money back. You know what? She had another woman hold me down."

Bernard felt a lump form in his throat. He didn't want to hear this. "Ma, you don't have to—"

Anna lowered herself to the couch. "I remember a cigarette hanging out of her mouth. This big, long ash dropped off it and onto me, and she just brushed it away. I could hardly breathe with all the smoke."

Reverend Grace moved to her side.

Anna wailed and tugged a circular-patterned quilt from the back of the couch and into her lap. Tears soaked into the triangular pieces of fabric as she looked wistfully at the surface. "That vile woman shoved a wire coat hanger into me. She killed my baby." Anna wrapped herself in the quilt and rocked again. "Then I passed out."

Bernard fell to his knees in front of his mother. "Ma, I'm sorry I couldn't protect you."

"You were too young."

"I would have fought for you."

"We hid it from you."

"Where was Dad? Why didn't he protect you?"

"When I woke, your father had carried me home and put me in bed."

"Were you all right?"

"I bled for two days before he got scared and took me to the hospital."

"I remember you being gone. Dad was yelling about you costing him more money." Bernard slowly shook his head as the realization sank in.

"They saved me, but the doctor said I'd never have more children." Anna reached out an arm from the confines of the quilt and stroked Bernard's head. "I cried when they told me, but your father was happy he wouldn't have to worry no more about extra mouths to feed."

Bernard groaned with the pain of the loss and humiliation his mother suffered at his father's hands.

"You're my joy, but I always wanted to have another baby . . . a little girl. A girl bonding with her momma is a special thing." Her eyes yearned for a better time.

"I'm sorry for your tragic experience, but there is hope. This is a new day," said Reverend Grace.

Anna glanced at him. "The church wouldn't help us. Turned us out is what they did. Said it was our punishment for killin' the baby. We walked away and ain't never gone back. In fact, shortly after, we moved here to Scranton."

Bernard looked at Reverend Grace. His face looked hopeful. Bernard wondered if things could really change after all that pain.

6

July 25, 1942

Cordelia trudged into the house, having survived the walk up the hill from the grocery store. Her arms hung limp, and beads of sweat snaked down her back. It was high noon, and even though the calendar read the twenty-fifth of July, the heat seared like the end of August.

The screen door slammed behind her before she thought to catch it. She winced and waited a moment, holding her breath. The top of her head radiated heat. Lucky for her, Grammy didn't see her without a hat. She reminded Cordelia frequently to wear one as the sun would give her wrinkles.

"Cordelia, is that you, baby girl?" Grammy Mae's voice drifted through the house.

She squeezed her eyes shut. Caught. "Yes, ma'am."

Cordelia wound her way through the dining room, grabbing a cardboard church fan from the table. She dropped the paper bag of potatoes and onions on the kitchen counter and reached for a glass to fill with cold tea. Mom used their tea ration to make iced tea. It went much further than making it by the single cup.

Cordelia scooped the aluminum tea ball out of the bottom of the tall glass pitcher, unscrewed the lid, dumped the used tea leaves in the garbage can, and tossed the ball in the sink.

She added a precious, scant teaspoon of sugar to the glass she poured and then reached in the freezer for a few ice cubes. Just this past spring the church Board had decided the pastor needed a brand-new refrigerator. Well, truth be told, her mother's harping at them had helped the cause, and right now Cordelia was enjoying the welcome frigid relief. Steam rose from her arm in the cold compartment. She lingered for a blissful second.

"Cordelia?"

"Coming, Grammy." She plunked the cubes in the glass. A wave of tea swirled around the intrusion, splashing over the sides and down across her fingers as she shut the refrigerator. She licked at her fingers. Grammy's summons gave a good enough reason to leave the tea ball unwashed at the moment.

She scampered into Grammy Mae's room with the sweating tea glass pressed against her neck.

Grammy sat in her rocker with Cordelia's quilt draped across her lap. Over the last few years Grammy had worked on it sporadically; but now it seemed every time Cordelia saw her, she was plugging away at it.

Grammy tacked in the new colors Cordelia had gathered to add. She wanted to remember forever one mistake, the paper bag parties. She hadn't told Grammy the reason for the tan material, but she was sure the wizened old woman knew.

"It's beautiful, Grammy!" She scanned the rows. The colors swirled in a kaleidoscope of color, marking beautiful memories of their time together. It comforted her to see so many of her grandmother's prayers represented by individual pieces of cloth. The more she sat with Grammy and explained her problems, the more Grammy taught her how to "pray rightly," as she called it. But it was like balancing on a fence, some days it helped her, and other days it seemed to be a useless exercise in talking to thin air.

"Come sit and work with me, child. My old fingers are tired today."

Cordelia eagerly seated herself on the stool beside the rocker, and accepted the folded square and threaded needle from her grandmother. "What are you praying for with this square?"

Grammy Mae stroked Cordelia's hair. "I was praying for a good friend to help you through the tough times."

Cordelia stopped in mid-stitch and frowned. "What good friend, and what tough times?"

"Well, I don't know, baby. That's just what the Lord laid on my heart."

Cordelia set about praying. She recalled the blue, green, and yellow stars on the red triangles of material from a summer jumper she wore several years ago. She prayed Grammy's request, but at the same time she prayed that the tough times didn't need to happen soon.

"I'm very proud of you, baby."

"Why, Grammy?" Cordelia stopped praying.

"Because you've taken to prayin' like you were born to it."

"It's only because of you." Cordelia savored the aura of peace, but she didn't know if it came from the prayers or from being with her grandmother.

"Well, that's as good a place to start as any." Grammy Mae flinched and squeezed her eyes shut for a moment.

Cordelia glanced at her. "Are you all right?"

"Just a touch of gas. There must have been a few green spots on that potato I fried for breakfast."

⁂

Cordelia planted her feet against the banister and pushed the porch swing. The wide legs of her pink gabardine slacks fluttered with the motion. She checked her watch for the tenth time in the last five minutes. Almost two o'clock. Bernard was late for their walk downtown to the Strand Theatre and the Saturday matinee of *Yankee Doodle Dandy*.

She understood his reluctance at arriving on time. He hated motion picture musicals, with all the dancing and hopping around. He called them girlie shows. She loved them for those same reasons. He liked cowboys and gangsters while she preferred musicals and Walt Disney. Cordelia sighed. What did they actually have in common?

She loved him desperately and completely. He had been her *Prince Charming* since the first time she met him. Well, maybe the fact that she'd watched *Snow White and the Seven Dwarves* about twenty times at the Comerford Theatre and *then* met him might have carried a little influence.

And she knew he loved her. He had stolen her first kiss and declared his love while they watched *Carson City Kid*, starring Roy Rogers, at the Riviera Theatre. Cordelia cocked her head. She realized a lot of their *moments* involved motion pictures.

Their love for the Lord was mutual, but sometimes she felt like a fraud. Grammy kept teaching her about the Lord, and she really tried to learn. A lot of it just didn't make sense. It seemed like just a lot of noise in the air.

Shallow—her faith seemed as thin as the veneer layer on the living room radio and felt just as cheap as the fake wood. She and Bernard were almost the same age, yet Bernard's love for the Lord was natural, like breathing, even in the face of all the evil and meanness he'd experienced. How could someone of his age have such strong faith?

She checked her watch as he waltzed around the corner. Cordelia stood and leaned over the white banister. "Hey, you're going to make us late."

"I think we ought to wait till next week to go." He took the porch stairs two at a time.

Cordelia feigned displeasure by pursing her lips. "What do you mean? I've been waiting for this motion picture to open since I saw the previews." She plopped back on the swing and crossed her arms over her chest.

Bernard sat down beside her, wrapped his right arm around her shoulders, and used his long legs to propel the swing. "Listen, sugar babe, I think we should stay away from the Strand today. I've heard some talk there might be a rumble around there."

"Who said that?" Cordelia frowned.

"The guys at the basketball game this morning said some Wilkes-Barre boys are mad because one of our Scranton boys is dating a girl from down their way. She apparently was going with one of the high school jocks, and now he's out for revenge."

"What's that got to do with us?"

"I just don't want you around any disagreeable situations." Bernard nuzzled her neck. "I would be very angry if anyone hurt my sugar babe."

Cordelia scrunched her shoulder to her ear, but the shivers running down her spine from his warm breath made it hard to concentrate on her annoyance. "Do you promise to take me next week?"

"Promise," said Bernard, as he exhaled slowly into her ear.

She turned to him. "I think you're bribing me with your display of affections, mister."

A smile pulled on the right side of his lips. "Did I convince you?"

Cordelia closed her eyes and leaned her head back on his shoulder. "Yes, you did." She huffed a sigh. "How's your mom doing?"

Bernard stopped rocking the swing. "Where did that come from? Is this a mood killer because I won't take you to the movies?"

"No. I'm worried about her." She drew back a bit. Her mother might look out a window and see them, or heaven forbid, one of the neighbors mention it to her father. "It's only been a couple months since your mom admitted the abortion. You said she was distraught. I can't imagine how she feels."

"I think she's made peace with herself about the loss. Then she got additional grief because my father had a conniption fit about her telling your father. Dad's been a nightmare to live with ever since. He said our private business shouldn't have left the house, let alone be told to a nosy preacher." Bernard winced at repeating his father's word *nosy*.

"Are you still having Bible study with her when your father isn't home?" Cordelia had contemplated joining them. Bernard knew more about the Bible than she did, but it might be awkward for his mom. Then again, to admit in front of his mother that she was basically Bible illiterate? Besides, Bernard's father scared her. When she went to their house, she usually didn't enter further than the kitchen.

Bernard frowned. "Yes, we're making slow progress. I think I've shown her enough scriptures to convince her God still loves her, and she is progressing on forgiveness for herself. But I don't want to think what would happen if my father caught us studying. I'm glad he's taken on extra shifts at the mine."

"I will pray for her." The minute the words were out of her mouth Cordelia knew those were Grammy's words. More of Grammy's words popped into her head . . . *You only need a mustard seed of faith.* Well, her mustard seed was a half one.

Cordelia stared into Bernard's smoky gaze. His thick lashes cast shadows across his eyes. An adrenaline rush sparked in her chest and thoughts of his mom slipped away from her consciousness.

He looked down at her. The swing stopped rocking. His lips brushed across hers. Cordelia's heart pounded quite loudly. She was sure Bernard could hear it. She reached out her right hand and stroked his cheek. Bernard lifted her hand and kissed her palm.

Footsteps clicked on the hall floor on the other side of the screen door. Both teens jerked up straight. Bernard unwound his arm from Cordelia's shoulders. They rocked the swing, hands in their laps.

Betty Grace strolled onto the porch and gave them a knowing glance. Slung across her forearm was a chic white and yellow Bakelite pocketbook that matched her stacked-heel shoes. The bright yellow sundress, the requisite pearls, and a large yellow straw hat created the perfect outfit for an afternoon of shopping.

Cordelia smiled at her. "What's on your agenda this afternoon?" Everyone else seemed to save money like squirrels storing for winter while her mother lived in the world of fashion, oblivious to everything but her own shopping pleasures. Mother often remarked that as the first lady of the church she had standards to uphold. She railed on the inconvenience of war because her favorite items, like nylons, were in short supply. Cordelia believed her mother sided with her about the job because a clothing designer and seamstress would benefit her wardrobe.

"I'm going down Wyoming Avenue to the Globe Store, and I also need to swing around to Lackawanna Avenue and stop at Kresge's and A. S. Beck's. I might as well drop in at Woolworth's while I'm down that far. I'll be several hours," said Betty as she rummaged through the contents of her pocketbook. She retrieved a pair of pale yellow lace gloves.

Cordelia suppressed a smirk. While everyone else collected goods for the war effort, her mother collected price tags.

"Your father should be home in an hour or two. He had a business meeting at the church today with several elders he couldn't meet with during the week. Will you be here?"

Cordelia nodded. "I should be." She sometimes wondered if her father loved the church more than her mother. He spent all of his time there. She rarely saw them together, other than at church, putting on their Sunday faces.

Betty waved and headed off down the street.

As soon as her mother turned down Olive Street, Cordelia grabbed Bernard's hand. "Come on. Let's go sit in the backyard where the neighbors can't see us."

Bernard stayed seated. "I don't think that's the best of ideas. We could get into trouble."

Cordelia smiled and wiggled her eyebrows up and down. "I know. That's the general idea."

"No, we can sit right here. There's less temptation." He squirmed as though it wouldn't be too hard to convince him to move.

Cordelia slid closer to him and nuzzled against his neck. "But I wanted to be alone with you," she cooed.

Bernard took a deep breath. "I love you and would like nothing better than to be alone with you, but it's just more temptation than I think I could handle. Your father expects me to take care of you."

Cordelia flashed her sweetest smile and batted her eye-lashes. "But I really—"

"Bernard, oh, Bernard," said a lilting, syrupy voice.

Cordelia and Bernard turned to look over the banister. A slender woman wearing too much makeup and bright red nail polish on inch-long nails sashayed along the walkway, waving an arm full of noisy bracelets.

"Oh, great," said Bernard. He dropped back against the swing without acknowledging her.

"Bernard," said the woman in a singsong tone, "I just knew I'd find you out here on the Avenue." She slowly climbed the stairs in three-inch heels.

Cordelia glared at the intruder. "What do you want with *my* Bernard, Jasmine?" Jasmine Jackson, JJ to her friends, of which Cordelia did not consider herself, wore a wraparound white blouse tied high in the front. She allowed her midriff to show, paired with tight pink Capri pants that looked like they were painted on her twenty-year-old frame.

"Well, sugar," she batted her eyes at Cordelia, "Stoney needs Bernard to come and work on my car. I told him I knew where he'd be hiding on a Saturday afternoon, and I came right on down to fetch him." She leaned over the banister. Her cleavage threatened to spill from the confines of her blouse.

Would Bernard fall for JJ's open blouse? Cordelia glanced at Bernard. He looked down at his hands. She put her hand over his. "Well, he's busy. You can get your car worked on some other time." She set her jaw and stared JJ down. *If a looks could put you to sleep like Snow White . . .*

Bernard groaned and slid his hand out from under hers. "No, I have to go if Stoney wants me for work."

"Bernard, we were spending the afternoon together." Cordelia set her jaw.

JJ let a lazy smile slide cross her lips as she leaned against the banister and stretched out one leg in a modeling pose.

Cordelia felt the urge to move the smile to the back of JJ's head. *Did she just think about striking someone?* She thought about it for a hot second. *Yes, when it came to Bernard, she did feel the urge to defend her territory.*

Bernard stood. "I'm sorry, honey, but I have to go." He pecked her on the cheek and jogged down the stairs with JJ flouncing behind. Cordelia sat there with her mouth hanging open. He left at JJ's finger snap?

JJ stopped at the end of the walkway, grinned broadly at Cordelia, and waved before she scooted off around the corner behind Bernard.

Cordelia was ready to bite somebody. She kicked at the banister and winced as a pain shot from her toes to her calf. How could he go off with that hussy? She was as transparent as mom's tea glasses with her sashaying hips and long fingernails. Cordelia mumbled under her breath and rocked with as much force as emotion.

"You're gonna break that swing if you rock any harder."

Cordelia snapped from her irritation. Gertie Truitt leaned against the porch post with her legs crossed at the ankle. Cordelia had met Gertie at the beginning of the school's spring semester. She wasn't part of Cordelia's normal social circle and several people gave her a hard time about the friendship. But Gertie wasn't a shallow phony and Cordelia appreciated her.

"I'm really ticked off! Bernard just went back to work because *Miss* Jasmine Jean Jackson came looking for him." Cordelia bolted from the swing. "Can you imagine? We were sitting here minding *my* own business, not hers, and she comes swinging her hips, and batting her eyes—"

"Whoa, time out." Gertie held up both hands in surrender. "Calm down before you bust a gut."

"I'll calm down when I can put that woman on a slow boat to China."

Gertie sat on the swing and burst out laughing. "You're something else. I've never seen you this messed up over that man."

"Well, he doesn't usually do things with other girls to annoy me."

"The way I see it, you've got two options," said Gertie, as she stretched out her legs.

Cordelia plopped down and crossed her arms over her chest. "Like to punch her in the nose?" It sounded stupid saying it because she'd never struck another person in her entire life. But she might choose to change.

"One," Gertie lifted her pointer finger, "you can go back in the Court and watch him fix her car. Or two," Gertie grinned between her two fingers, "you can come downtown with me."

"What are you going to do downtown?" If Gertie was a shopper like Mom, Cordelia was *not* interested.

"I'm going to the Strand Theatre to see *Yankee Doodle Dandy*."

Cordelia sat up straight. A broad grin crossed her face. "I thought there was going to be trouble down there today."

Gertie shook her head. "Not that I heard of. What's supposed to be going on?"

Cordelia let her glance travel along the street in the direction Bernard had walked. "Bernard said there was going to be a rumble. I think we'd better stay home."

Gertie snickered. "Are you sure he didn't make that excuse to be here when she showed?"

"Bernard wouldn't do something like that."

"Are you sure? That's one loose woman chasing him. She's older too, at least twenty."

"Bernard loves me," said Cordelia with all the confidence she could muster. "Besides, he's a perfect gentleman. I've been trying to slap the make on him for the last fifteen minutes and I got nowhere."

Gertie motioned Cordelia off the porch and down the walkway. "That's the thing about men. They marry good girls, but that brazen hussy is the type they like to . . . well, she's the easy type."

Cordelia matched Gertie's longer gait. "Bernard would not do that to me. Would he?"

7

Cordelia walked beside Gertie as they strolled down Washington Avenue. Gertrude Truitt tested Cordelia's expanding friendship experiment. She worked through her misgivings and grimaced at the way she portrayed the new friendship, but it was the truth despite the tackiness. It was an experiment. Bernard called her a snob about her friends. It didn't help any that Grammy agreed with him. Cordelia understood the need to expand beyond her comfort circle. She just wasn't sure how successful she'd be at it.

They approached Central High School on the corner of Vine Street and Washington Avenue. Cordelia stared at the ornate stone carvings. "This is a really neat building. I wish we could go to school here."

"You only have one more year. It wouldn't be worth it now to switch, even if you could."

Cordelia turned to look at Gertie. "What do you mean *you could*? Don't you mean *we*?"

Gertie focused her attention further down the street. "I went in and filed the papers. I'm not going back in September."

"No! Why did you do that?" Cordelia grabbed her arm to stop her.

Gertie smiled, removed her hand, and motioned her forward. "I took a summer job at the sewing factory. They're paying good money and they offered me full-time work." Gertie shook her head. "I can't afford to miss out on that kind of employment."

"But you only have a year left." Cordelia's words echoed off the mountainous stone block front of the Masonic temple.

"And then what? I go to one more year of school and then I can graduate and get the job in the factory. No, by this time next year I could be flush with a few bucks." Gertie's words also echoed off the building, as though being swatted.

Cordelia bit down on her bottom lip. Gertie was right. She'd get the same manual labor job whether she finished school or not. That was the nature of the times. "I'm just going to miss you."

"You'll still see me. I misjudged you when we started hanging out. I worried your friendship with me was some sort of joke among you and your friends. I thought you wanted something," said Gertie.

Almost to Mulberry Street, Cordelia measured her words. Their friendship had blossomed in the spring, and now she was confident of their bond. *How do I say this right?* "I do want something from you."

They crossed the intersection, and Gertie stopped in front of the municipal building. Her face went sober as she tipped her chin down. "What do you want?"

"I want you to help me be a better person."

"Girl! You scared the sweat right off me! I thought you were serious." Gertie increased her stride again.

"I am!" Cordelia jogged to catch up to her. "I'm ashamed of my behavior and it took a couple of other people telling me I was a *light-skinned snob* for the reality to sink in."

"You're serious? Who would talk to you about that?"

"My Grammy, for one," Cordelia smiled. "She's taught me a whole bunch of stuff the last few months, like accepting other people for who they are and how to appreciate prayer." She didn't see her father spending as much time in prayer as Grammy did. Who was right? Following her father's ideas would be a lot less work.

Gertie attended the same church. She knew Cordelia's grandmother was a church elder. "That old lady's as sharp as a tack. I heard my ma say she was a prayer warrior, but I didn't care or understand enough at the time to know what it meant."

"It's kinda embarrassing to say that I'm a PK and still don't see what prayer could accomplish."

"Preachers' kids don't have the market cornered on stupid." Gertie stopped.

Cordelia raised her eyebrows with her best serious look, then burst into laughter again.

Gertie released a held breath. "I'm very sorry. I did *not* mean it the way it sounded." They reached Linden Street and crossed over to the other side of Washington Avenue as they hurried to the cinema.

"I'm trying to decide which is worse . . . being called 'stupid' or 'high yella.'"

"Okay, let's go back to the high yella part. It feels good for me to get this off my chest, too," said Gertie. "I've spent my whole life in class warfare with high yellas acting like they were better than us darker-skinned girls." She looked embarrassed at using the derogatory name as an ordinary word.

Cordelia shrugged. Gertie didn't feel that way about her. "I was really scared to make friends with you. I thought you were going to beat me up like *they* did when I was young."

"*They?*"

Cordelia lowered her eyes and watched her feet travel the pavement. "The Wilson kids."

Gertie snapped her fingers. "Hey, I remember them! Those kids were bad with a capital B. Girl, I'll tell ya, they even beat me."

Cordelia and Gertie broke into snorts and giggles.

"I'm glad we're friends. I really resent my old gang for trying to dictate my friendships." Cordelia took a swipe at the beads of sweat collecting on her forehead.

Gertie was moving like she meant to make that matinee on time. "I've had a couple of my friends accuse you of slumming for being friends with me."

"Well, don't that beat all? At least they don't want to chase me down the street." Cordelia made a face. "I wondered if that's because of the war. Everybody's more patriotic, especially since all the older guys had to sign with Selective Service. Pearl Harbor sort of puts a whole new priority on life, knowing you might have to go to war."

They turned the corner onto Spruce. The Strand Theatre stood in the middle of the block, directly across the street from the Ritz Theatre. Scranton had a treasure trove of motion picture theatres.

"Speaking of war, there could be a problem," said Gertie. She motioned down the street to a couple of dozen kids, mostly boys, in a heated discussion.

Cordelia spotted her friend Marcie Ballenger. She and two other girls pressed against the ticket booth in the Strand doorway. They looked afraid to walk past the argument.

Marcie spotted Cordelia and waved to her, pleading for help.

A loud argument erupted from the gathered group of boys. A heavyset guy shoved a tall blonde kid. His offense? He wore Tech's red and white. But another guy in Wilkes-Barre's G.A.R. blue and gray pulled the heavy guy back. The argument escalated, with finger jabs instead of punches for the moment.

Cordelia studied the disagreeable group. "I know those girls stuck in the doorway. Do you think we dare get them out of there?" Gertie was taller and broader, and outweighed her by at least forty pounds.

Gertie eyed the helpless light-skinned girls and snickered. "Yeah, I guess we could rescue them." She started toward the group.

Cordelia hurried to stay right beside her. Her heart pounded. *What was she thinking?* Stick like glue to Gertie! They moved through the outer ring of the crowd.

"Oh, Cordelia, please help us get out of here. They're even arguing inside. They started throwing popcorn," said Marcie.

Gertie shook her head, "Babies." She motioned and ran interference as the three girls hurried away with them.

About ten feet from the crowd, Marcie hugged Cordelia. "Thank you for saving us from those rowdies."

"Don't thank me! Gertie got you out of there." Cordelia looked at each of them in turn. "I wouldn't have come down this street by myself."

Gertie stood stone-faced, staring at the three girls.

Marcie looked at Gertie, and then lowered her eyes to the ground. "Um, thank you for getting us out of there." With that, she and the other two girls hurried off along the street.

Cordelia's mouth dropped open. "If that ain't a piece of work. Their response was about as rude as it could possibly get. I guess I'm beginning to see the light."

"That's all right," said Gertie. "I'm used to them being rude."

"Well, I'm not," said Cordelia as she turned. She glanced across the street to the front of the Ritz Theatre and spotted a familiar man.

The man emptied garbage cans into the theatre's trash receptacle. Cordelia looked again. "Are you seeing what I'm seeing?"

Gertie looked in the same direction. "Yeah, isn't that Bernard's father?"

"Yes, it is, but he's supposed to be working an extra shift in the mines today. What is going on here?" She stepped into the street.

Gertie grabbed her arm. "Hold it, girlfriend. You can't confront your boyfriend's father and ask him what he's doing. I know you're getting your bravery badge today. But it doesn't include confronting fathers."

Cordelia looked behind them. A beat cop came from the other direction. "I think it's time to go."

She pursed her lips, then added, "Maybe you're right about Mr. Howard. But at least I can tell Bernard. What does this mean? What's he doing down here when he's supposed to be in the mines?"

8

Bernard fiddled with the pulley to tighten the fan belt. Next, he tried to loosen the adjustment. JJ hopped onto the driver's side running board, and the jostle caused the wrench to slip off the bolt and gouge the knuckle of his other hand. He inhaled, holding onto the breath and the words that wanted to spill out. The wrench clattered through the engine compartment and landed underneath the car.

Bernard was uncomfortable alone in the garage with this female barracuda. But Stoney had handed him the keys and told him to lock the place after he finished with JJ's Chevy. She needed the fan belt tightened and a new directional contact socket for her taillights. The part came in on Monday, but she never showed to get it replaced.

He flicked his wrist to disperse the pain. Out of the corner of his eye, Bernard saw JJ move from the running board and sit on the low crate next to the automobile. She crossed her legs and assumed a pose against the driver's side suicide door. He brought the bloody knuckle to his mouth.

"How long do you think this job will take?" JJ leaned her arms onto the huge fender around the engine compartment. Six inches separated her from Bernard.

He refused to look at her, but he could swear she blew in his ear.

Bernard moved away and reached under the hood from a different angle. "Should be about an hour, give or take." Fifteen minutes, if she'd stop invading his space. Bernard bit his tongue. The 1940 Special Deluxe Town Sedan was really sweet. But the customer was really sour. Her family owned expensive automobiles, and she was one of Stoney's best-paying customers. He'd be upset if Bernard lost her business.

"How long you been working on cars, Bernard?" She leaned in further.

"Long enough." Bernard raised a hand. "Hang back there. You're going to get in a mess of grease."

JJ giggled and swiped the rag from Bernard's back pocket.

His head jerked as the fabric zipped out, and he hit the open hood. "Ow! You need to back up to let me work." He rubbed the lump rising on his forehead.

"Oh, I'm sorry, Bernard. Let me look at it for you." She moved toward him with her hand outstretched.

Bernard ducked back out of reach. "Stop! I need to work here."

JJ smiled. "Okay, I'll let you work. I was just going to look at it. Listen, let me make it up to you."

Bernard went back to work without answering. He wanted to get this job done and get out of here.

"My mom's got a 1937 Ford, and the thing is quite per-snickety. It refuses to start. I know Stoney could tow it in for us. But if you could come over to the house and fix it, we'd pay you a whole ten dollars for the work."

Bernard's ears pricked. Ten dollars! He'd have to work three days for that kind of pay. He peered out from under the hood. "Sure, I'd be glad to come over and fix your ma's Ford. I've worked on that one before."

"You're a real peach." JJ reached for Bernard, her right foot caught on the crate. She squeaked as she fell forward.

⎯⎯⎯

Cordelia strode down Dix Court. How would she tell Bernard about seeing his father? He needed to know something wasn't right. Bernard hadn't mentioned his dad working at the Ritz. Wait. Did he need to know or was she nosing around for a chance to see what *Miss* JJ might do with her boyfriend?

She slowed. How was she going to explain *why* she had wandered down Spruce Street in the first place? Bernard had refused to take her because of the danger. Admitting she went would create problems of its own.

The garage door hung open. *Good, Bernard was there. Or was that bad? She needed an explanation for being downtown. Walk slower or think faster.*

"Bernard," she yelled as she reached the doorway. She stepped into the cool work space. The heavy scent of motor oil perfumed the air like a mechanic's incense. Her eyes adjusted from the bright outside light to the diffuse interior illumination. "Bernard—"

There on the floor, in front of the Alameda green metallic Chevy, lay Bernard with JJ rolling around on top of him.

Cordelia stared. Her mind went blank. She let out a scream.

Both whipped their heads in the direction of the shriek.

Bernard pushed JJ off him and she hit the ground with a resounding thud.

JJ rolled partly under her car. She pushed with her hands and slid in the excess grease at the edge of the pit. She cursed like a storm trooper.

"What do you mean by getting this goop all over my new outfit?" Her hands slid again in the lubricant. She crawled far enough away from the car to find a dry patch and managed to stand. A splotch of yellow-gold axle grease streaked a line down her left sleeve.

Cordelia swallowed a giggle at the sight of oil from the garage floor soaking into JJ's tight pants. *Serves her right!*

JJ straightened. The spreading patches on her knees looked like painted-on kneepads.

Cordelia furrowed her brow at the dirty demon and wished her into the grease pit under the car. Then she turned her sights on Bernard.

"Cordelia, this is not what it looks like." Bernard scrambled to his feet.

"You bet it isn't, mister. Because what it was *supposed* to look like was you fixing a car," fumed Cordelia, "not playing rolling pins with Miss Tight Pants." She glared at JJ, who offered a sly smile back.

Cordelia growled, spun on her heels, and marched toward the open door.

"Honey, let me explain." Bernard reached for her arm.

She jerked her elbow out of his hand. "Don't you dare touch me!"

He backed away.

JJ moved to his side. "Don't worry about her, Bernard. She doesn't deserve you."

Cordelia's eyes widened and she released a guttural scream. "You . . . you keep him!"

She stormed out of the garage. The sun blinded her for a moment and she tripped on a broken glass bottle. She caught herself. Pain shot through her sandaled foot as she looked down. Blood oozed from the side of her big toe. She hobbled along the Court, grumbling under her breath.

—∞—

Bernard tried to follow after her, but JJ pulled him back by his shirttail. He struggled to remove it from her grasp. "Let go of me, woman. What is your problem?" He jerked the material from her hand and heard a rip. Bernard shut his eyes and counted. Just what he needed, another ripped shirt. The engine block pulley had taken care of his other good one on Monday.

"I need to talk to Cordelia." Bernard carefully edged JJ aside.

"Hey, I need my automobile finished. Stoney said you would have it done so I could go to dinner with my folks." She looked at her watch. "It's getting real close to that time." She leaned back against her car and struck her signature model pose.

Bernard hurried to the doorway. "Cordelia," he yelled. "Come back. Let me explain."

Cordelia was too far down the alley for him to catch her before she made it home, and she didn't look back.

Bernard leaned against the doorway. *Now what do I do, Lord?*

9

Cordelia stormed in the front door. The screen's slam was satisfying. *Grammy will just have to yell. I'm too upset.* She walked around the living room in circles. How could he do this to me? Maybe Gertie was right. Maybe men wanted different kinds of women for marrying and for hanky-panky. She stomped her foot. A pain stabbed her bloodied toe. She winced. She wanted to be everything to him. Why hadn't her mother told her about these things?

A tear slid down her cheek. More frustration than rage coursed through her blood, more pain than anger. What was she supposed to do other than love him? Grammy would know the answer.

Cordelia wiped the wet mess from her face and shook her head to compose herself. She would try to be adult about this when she talked to Grammy.

Cordelia stopped in the kitchen to dab at her toe with a moistened dish towel. It had stopped bleeding. Grammy hadn't yelled at her about the screen door slamming. Maybe she was napping.

Cordelia tapped lightly on the closed door. "Grammy, are you awake?"

No answer.

She knocked again, a little harder. "Grammy, it's me."

No answer.

Cordelia turned the knob slowly and quietly. She peeked in. Grammy Mae sat in her rocker with her eyes closed. Cordelia's Pinecone Quilt was spread across her lap, and a needle was in one hand, a blue square in the other.

How sweet. She fell asleep working on the quilt. She had complained lately that her fingers and eyes weren't working like they used to. She'd often joke with Cordelia that after eighty-nine everything seemed to fall apart.

Cordelia smiled. The disagreement with Bernard would have to wait until Grammy woke. They could talk after dinner while she helped work on the quilt during their special time together. In the last few years, she'd grown closer to Grammy Mae than she was to her mother. Her mother seemed a little jealous of the relationship between her daughter and her mother-in-law. But what could she do about that?

She backed out of the doorway, turned the knob to retract the latch, and released the handle. She moved to walk away but stopped. An image registered—a wet spot on the floor.

She opened the door again. Under Grammy's rocker a big puddle spread. Grammy must have wet herself. Cordelia moved to the rocker. Should she wake her? She couldn't let her sit in wet clothes, but by the same token Grammy might be embarrassed to have her granddaughter see her with soiled clothing.

Cordelia stood there a second, but the internal debate ended when a prickle of fear rolled down her back. Something felt off. Grammy didn't look right up close. Cordelia's heart started to pound. "Gram. Grammy, wake up!"

She bent forward. Grammy looked like a wax doll. Cordelia reached out her hand, but mere inches from Grammy's hand she pulled back. Grammy's chest hadn't moved.

"Grammy!" Cordelia touched her arm. Her arm was already growing cool. The skin that had been soft and supple was waxy and lifeless. Tears flooded Cordelia's eyes, rolled down her cheeks, and splashed on Grammy's hand and on the quilt.

Cordelia screamed in anguish and fell to the floor at her grandmother's feet. "Grammy, come back. Please come back. I can't do this without you." If she reasoned with Grammy, reasoned with God, Grammy would come back. Life would go on like normal. She could tell Grammy about Bernard acting up and ask what to do.

"Grammy, please," she wailed, rubbing Grammy's hand as though she could transfer the life from her own body into her grandmother's.

"God, don't take her. Please don't take her. I'll do anything you want." Her shoulders shook with sobs. "Just give me another chance. Grammy, please come back."

She touched her grandmother's face. "No, God, don't do this to me. Please, please give her back." Cordelia willed Grammy's eyes to open, willed her to smile, and call her sugar babe.

Grammy Mae's face was cold.

Cordelia screamed a low guttural sound. Gone. Her beloved grandmother was gone. Cordelia's world had lost its light.

"Why, God? No one loves me like Grammy. You're leaving me all alone . . . all alone." She pulled her knees to her chest, wrapped her arms around them, and rocked. She half expected an audible answer. Grammy always said God talked to her. If Grammy could hear God, why wasn't she hearing him, especially after screaming? She knew he could hear her.

"God, are you listening? I'm scared. Grammy was the only one I had to talk to. No one else understands me." Bernard. She loved him, but it wasn't the same. He didn't understand the ways of women.

"I don't know all the answers without Grammy to explain." Many times Grammy had talked her through decisions.

Cordelia stared at the rag rug. The only sound . . . Grammy's clock on the dresser. Tick. Tick. Tick. Gone. Gone. Gone.

She looked at Grammy's chest again and willed the slightest movement of life. Nothing but the tick. Tick. Tick.

Her face contorted in rage and she slammed her fists into the floor. "No! Why do you hate me? I can't make it alone."

—⁂—

Cordelia lost track of time. Ten minutes? An hour? She cried herself dry, until there were no more tears left in her soul to wash away the anguish that claimed her. Her hands were bruised and sore.

She removed the needle and cloth square, and folded Grammy's hands, one on top of the other. She sat at the foot of the chair with her head resting on the quilt draped across her grandmother's lap.

The screen door closed. Footsteps pounded through the living room and into the kitchen. Heavy, male, not her mother's heels.

"Daddy!" Weak from crying, her voice cracked. She tried again, "Daddy, come here!"

"Cordelia, why do you sound like—" Her father, Emanuel Grace, stood in the doorway. His glance traveled over the scene. The light faded from his eyes. He suddenly seemed smaller as his shoulders slumped.

Cordelia raised her head, her eyes gritty and raw from crying gallons of tears. "Grammy's gone, Dad." A lone tear rolled down her cheek as her lip quivered.

She scrambled to her feet and launched herself into her father's arms.

He ran his hand across his eyes. "Lord, take care of my mother. I hope she had a glorious homecoming. She's kinda bossy. You may have to give her a couple jobs to keep her busy enough. But Lord, she was a good woman, and she loves you."

His frame slumped and he moved, taking Cordelia with him, to sit on the edge of Grammy Mae's bed. He patted his daughter's back as he stared at his mother's lifeless shell.

"When did this happen?" Emanuel lifted her chin with his hand.

"I'm not sure. She was gone when I got home." Cordelia swallowed hard to force down the lump in her throat. "What time is it?"

Emanuel pulled out his pocket watch. "It's five forty-five. Where's your mother?"

"She went downtown around two o'clock."

Emanuel shook his head and muttered, "Probably spending money we don't have."

Where did that come from, at a time like this? Cordelia wanted to chalk it up to emotions, but it stuck with her. Dad never spoke of her mother that way. She ducked her head as she felt her cheeks heating. Grammy always shushed divisive talk. But Grammy was gone. This was a changing day.

Cordelia wanted to reach for the quilt. But she wanted things to stay the same. She wanted time to never move further from this moment. Grammy would point out that Cordelia wanted, wanted, wanted. But *want* wouldn't make things happen.

The clock ticked. Time moved.

Grammy was big on marking moments in Cordelia's life with spaces on the quilt. Her throat tightened. Did she have the mental strength to add this moment to her life covering?

She reached to touch the quilt. Her father released his hold on her shoulder and his hand slid down to rest on her back. She could feel his warmth through her blouse. Grammy used to rest her hand on her back, too, but now that wouldn't happen again. She stopped with her hand in midair.

"What's the matter?" Her father sounded defeated, lost, his voice lacking its normal rich ring of confidence.

"Grammy taught me to add life moments to my quilt and I thought . . ." Her voice trailed off to a whimper. A lump invaded her throat. "I was thinking I should add her passing . . ."

"There's time. You're just starting to grieve. I know you want to do something, but maybe it'd be better to leave that until later. You may want to go through her things and find the right material for the memory."

Cordelia watched him. "That's the first time I've ever heard you talk like you know what a Pinecone Quilt is all about."

Her father's smile seemed forced, sad. "I also grew up on your grammy's knee. She was my mother, remember?"

"Well, yes, I know." Cordelia swiveled to face him. "But you never let on you understood. I mean, all the times that Mom called it silly—"

"Your mom's heart is in the right place. She doesn't understand the sentiment. Her family traditions are different." He gulped. "With Mom's passing, our tradition ends."

Cordelia bolted upright. "No it won't! Grammy taught me everything. I can do this. I can carry it on . . . for her. Nothing has to change."

"Unfortunately there's a whole lot that needs to change."

Cordelia's chest tightened. The lump came back to her throat.

"No. I don't mean about the quilting. I mean about a bunch of other stuff. My mother's passing shows me our tomorrows are never guaranteed."

"Daddy?"

"Never you mind, baby girl. This'll all work out."

Her father had never called her that before. God had heard her after all.

10

July 27, 1942

Cordelia's next two days passed in a blur of friends, food, and all things fried. Tables full of foodstuffs declared a war with rationing. Plates, bowls, and trays of food covered every surface in the kitchen. Ironic with this feast, the mood should have been festive instead of somber.

The funeral home brought Grammy's body home for the wake.

Cordelia approached the living room doors. She didn't remember another occasion when the pocket doors had ever been closed. She pulled on the brass handles and the heavy dark maple doors slid silently back into the wall on either side.

Sadness engulfed her. Grammy lay in a coffin against the far wall of the living room. Cordelia couldn't bear it. She could never again enjoy this room with her family. She would always see Grammy in her lavender dress. She squeezed her eyes shut. When she opened them, she tried to focus on the flowers.

The walls on either side of the casket were smothered in gladiolus arrangements. Buckets of white spikes with red spots on the throat called Mibloom sat on multiple small podiums. Those were Grammy's favorites. More containers of ruffled creamy white glads with a red dart on the throat called

Perfume, which happened to be Mom's favorite. The living room looked like a florist shop explosion. Several fans ran to dispel the summer heat, but still the smell overpowered her. The flowers Cordelia once considered fragrant now smelled putrid. The odor made her gag.

Most of the adults sat in groups of two or three. They rejoiced in Grammy's home-going. A few sobbed faintly.

Cordelia heard one of the church elders in the hallway make a hushed announcement: "The criers are the usual professional mourners."

What did that mean? Cordelia'd never been to a funeral before. Her life had crashed. How would she put it back together? Dad's time was full of burial preparations. Mom didn't seem to have the time to talk her through it or consider her emotions. Neither had spent any real time with her in the last couple of days. Was she invisible? Grammy always helped her understand the world. Something had changed inside, as though her emotions had scabbed over like a scraped knee.

Cordelia turned to leave the room. Her tangled mind cleared for a moment. She turned back to the coffin. Her quilt, Cordelia's quilt, covered Grammy. No! Her mouth flew open in a guttural cry. She charged forward through the rows of chairs.

Her mother intercepted her, blocking the way. "What's the meaning of this? You should be on your best behavior, instead of running around like a banshee."

She took in Cordelia's appearance. "And for heaven's sake, go put on your Sunday clothes. Have you no respect for the dead?"

Cordelia tried to reach around her mother, fingers clawing at thin air. "That's my quilt. Grammy's is in her steamer trunk." Cordelia's mind fractured and shot in ten directions at once. She couldn't lose her quilt too. Her breathing turned into gulps as she reached for it.

Her mother grabbed her by the arm.

"Oh, Lord, give me strength," said her mom. "It doesn't really matter whose it is."

"Yes, it does!" Cordelia's voice rose. She wrenched her arm free.

One of the criers stopped in mid-sob to watch. Betty clenched her teeth. "Young lady, you're making a scene. I want you to stop it right now." She put her hands on both hips.

Cordelia took the unfettered moment to snatch the quilt. It snagged on the side handle as she turned to run. She felt the resistance.

Her mother lunged for the coffin.

Cordelia flicked the quilt. The material popped loose from the handle. She ran through the dining room clutching the quilt to her chest.

Her mother chased behind.

The tension from her pounding heart, and the tussle with her mother, caused her to gulp air. Dizzy, Cordelia ran into Grammy's room. She slammed the door shut and slid the lock into place. Hugging the quilt, she leaned against the door as she forced her breathing to normal.

Bang! She flinched.

"You open this door and give me that stupid quilt. You've made me a laughingstock in front of these people with your bad behavior."

Cordelia held the quilt tight to her chest. "Go away. I'm not coming out."

"We'll see about that. Wait till I find your father." The footsteps receded.

Cordelia glanced around the room. Her mouth dropped open. Grammy died two days ago and already the room was stripped bare of her possessions. Cardboard boxes rested in a pile on one side of the room. Dresser drawers hung open and the closet door stood ajar.

She peered in the dresser, then checked each piece of furniture. Nothing but the lining paper in the bottoms of the drawers remained. Even Grammy's brushes, combs, and dressing table tray were gone.

Cordelia's hands shook as she laid her precious quilt on Grammy's stripped bed. She rested her hand on the quilt. It took until this very hour for her to feel how much it meant to her. The quilt represented all that Grammy meant to her.

With this new recognition an awakening of sorts, she shut her eyes and smiled. Grammy would be pleased she had finally discovered the meaning of the quilt.

She wrestled the boxes from atop the steamer trunk and threw open the lid. The quilt wasn't easy to find under the pile. Cordelia found the corner of Grammy's quilt and hauled it out from between the compacted layers. She spread it out on the bed. Had she damaged it by pulling it out of the trunk?

Loose triangles dangled near the center of the quilt. Her hand ran across several of the disconnected spots. She pulled the quilt closer for a better inspection. The seams were loose. Cordelia fingered the threads, and counted the spots. A dozen triangles hung almost free. How did this happen? They weren't torn. The threads were pulled out. She rummaged through the top tray of the steamer trunk and found a needle and thread, then plopped onto the bed to repair the triangles.

Cordelia felt as though Grammy was guiding her hand. She relaxed, her breathing steadied, and by the time she finished patching the stitches on the last spot, she was humming. She inspected her work. She had matched the original work stitch for stitch. No one would be able to tell it had been disturbed. Grammy would be proud.

Cordelia gathered the quilt and brought it close to her face. She inhaled. She could smell Grammy. The perfume of her favorite sachet permeated the fabric. The familiar scent soothed Cordelia's raw heart.

If she spirited Grammy's quilt away and hid it, she'd be able to hold Grammy forever. She hung her head. That wasn't fair. Grammy told her more than once she couldn't have the quilt. It was Grammy's life covering.

Cordelia dropped it into her lap. She had to let Grammy and her quilt go.

Cordelia folded the two quilts and walked back into the living room. She looked around, ready for an argument. No Mom. Taking a deep breath to steel her resolve, Cordelia approached the coffin. With gentle fingers, she covered Grammy and tucked in the edges. Her hand rested on top of the quilt where Grammy's hands were folded.

She lowered her head and closed her eyes. Her tongue was plastered to the roof of her mouth. She couldn't speak words, but her mind talked. *Lord, give me the strength to get through this.* Her own prayer, heartfelt and genuine, and not a copy of what Grammy said or did. The numbness lifted and a gradual calm rolled over her.

Cordelia raised her head. Strange. She could almost hear Grammy telling her that it would be all right.

———

Cordelia sat curled in her unfinished quilt on the back porch swing. She couldn't deal with the adults inside and the creepiness of Grammy's body in the living room. Every time she went through the living room, she kept her head down and her eyes straight ahead.

Her mother stuck her head out around the screen door. "Gertie Truitt is here. Do you want to see her?"

"Yes, ma'am." She lowered the quilt from her shoulders. It was too hot to be wrapped in the quilt, especially outside in the humid July heat. But through the quilt, Grammy wrapped her arms around Cordelia's shoulders.

Gertie tromped through the kitchen and out the back door. She patted Cordelia on the shoulder as she passed her to sit on the other end of the swing. "I'm sorry for your loss."

"She's not lost. I know where she is." Cordelia managed a painful smile.

Gertie winced. "I didn't mean to be rude. I just don't know what to say. I've never had anybody in my family die."

"You're lucky. Grammy is my first time." Cordelia pulled the quilt close again. "Have you ever been to a funeral?"

Gertie shook her head. "No, and I don't think I like all those people crying." She reached over and touched the quilt. "Is this the quilt you said your Grammy was making for you?"

"Yes, and I had to fight with my mother to keep it." Cordelia bolted straight up.

"Why?" Gertie examined the stitch work along the outside row.

"She tried to put it in the coffin with Grammy. I took it back." Cordelia's eyes widened. "I tried to tell her that Grammy had her own, but she wouldn't listen."

"I saw the colorful one on her as I came through the living room." Gertie shuddered visibly. "I thought that was the one you two had been working on."

"That one is Grammy's. I had to go find it in her stuff." She held out the unfinished edge. "Now I have to finish mine on my own. I'm not sure I can."

"Sure you could." Gertie raised the edge and looked at the triangles. "This is just like the one my mom made for me. I've helped make my quilt and quilts for my two sisters."

Cordelia perked up. "Would you be willing to help me? I have to confess, I didn't pay enough attention to what Grammy was doing to be able to finish this on my own."

"Sure, that's what friends are for."

Cordelia mentally ran through her friends list. This girl, who she wouldn't have taken the time to be friends with a year ago, was the only person with enough depth to work on a quilt. "Emotionally shallow" described the rest of Cordelia's friends. How had that happened? And not one came to offer condolences.

"Do you have a lot of squares already cut?"

Cordelia looked stricken. "The stuff was in Grammy's room. It's all been packed." She dropped her feet from the swing. "I didn't even think of it. Come help me."

"Help you? Help you what?" Gertie dutifully followed behind Cordelia, down the hall and into the back bedroom.

Cordelia scanned the boxes. She opened the tops.

"What are we doing?" Gertie moved the boxes Cordelia shoved aside.

Cordelia accented her points by counting her fingers. "Grammy had a whole bunch of squares cut for the quilt, and more backing material, and all the threads and needles, and her shears and stuff." She held out four fingers.

She rummaged through a couple of boxes, pushing aside the contents as she looked for material. Her hand came to rest on Grammy's Bible. She plucked it from the bottom of a box.

"Where's all this stuff going?" Gertie looked around, her glance coming to rest on Grammy's Bible in Cordelia's hands.

"I don't know, but—"

"It's all going to Sally's as soon as the funeral is over," said her mother, who stood in the doorway. "I need this room."

"You're going to give all of Grammy's stuff to the Salvation Army? How could you? Don't you think there might be stuff I'd want to keep, like her Bible?" Cordelia held out the worn, leather-covered book. "You didn't even give me a chance to go through it."

"I've been through every stitch of her stuff, and believe me, there's nothing of value in any of it."

Cordelia stared at her. "We don't have the same taste in valuables. I want to keep Grammy's Bible and probably some other things." She tucked the hand holding the book behind her as though her mother might snatch it like she tried to do with the quilt.

"Help yourself," her mother said with a dismissive swing of her hand. She turned and walked back to the kitchen.

Gertie compressed her lips.

"What?" Cordelia glared at her.

"I don't want to say," said Gertie. "She's your mom. I'd be disrespectful."

"Grammy and Mom were not the best of friends." Cordelia placed the Bible on the bed and rooted through the boxes in earnest. She found the box of sewing supplies and quilt parts.

"Here, carry this." She handed Gertie the Bible and her quilt. Then she hoisted the box into her arms and stepped into the hall.

"Wait! Are you going to walk through the wake carrying that box?" Gertie looked like she'd rather have a tooth pulled with rusty pliers than walk back through the wake.

Cordelia grimaced. "I guess that's a bad idea. Let's walk around front."

She directed Gertie out the back door, around the house, and through the front door. They bypassed the living room for a straight line to Cordelia's. Once inside, Cordelia closed the door. She sat down on her bed and offered Gertie a seat beside her. She sorted through the box while Gertie leafed through Grammy's Bible.

"Your grammy had a lot of papers and things underlined in here," said Gertie as she flipped pages.

"Yeah, Grammy was always making notes in her Bible. That used to make my mom crazy. She said writing in a holy book was a personal affront to God." Cordelia giggled.

"I don't think God cares one way or the other," said Gertie. "I guess the important part to him is that you actually open it."

Cordelia nodded her head. "It was just one more thing for them to argue about."

"Your gram underlined a bunch of verses that have gemstones in them, like rubies, emeralds, diamonds, and sapphires. Wonder why?"

"I don't know. I never had a chance to talk to her much about the Bible. Actually, I avoided those conversations. They were boring." Cordelia looked over and then back at the box she rummaged through. "I was pretty stupid not to take more time with her. But now it's too late."

"It's never too late when it comes to the Bible."

"You sound like Grammy."

Gertie laughed. "Nah, I just grew up learning my Bible."

"I gotta say I ran from it. You never know what you have until it's gone." She shook her head.

"Speaking of gone . . . have you seen Bernard the last couple days?"

Cordelia's head jerked up from peering in the box. "No, I didn't see him at church yesterday. After the service Mom hustled me out of there to help her clean for today. Why do you ask?"

Gertie gulped hard and avoided eye contact with her.

Cordelia squared her gaze on Gertie. "You started this. Now answer me."

"I saw him yesterday."

"Okay, give me the skinny."

"He was walking along the driveway to JJ Jackson's house." Gertie's forehead started to sweat.

Cordelia froze, but thankfully, so did the scream in her throat. She bit down hard on her tongue. Her mother would have a fit if she disturbed their guests. Pin prickles stung her eyes. But there were no more tears left over after Grammy. Her heart sank into her stomach. Why? What did that vile woman have that she didn't have . . . besides sex appeal and risqué clothing?

—∞∞∞—

Cordelia put her hands to her face. *This is just a bad dream.*

A knock sounded at the door.

"Yes, who is it?" Cordelia lowered her hands and sighed. Gertie sat leafing through the Bible.

"Bernard is here to see you. I told him to wait on the front porch," said her mother. She leaned in the door and looked over at Gertie. "How many of your friends are coming around?"

Gertie glanced up from the Bible. "I guess I'd better be leaving."

"No, don't go. You just got here. I thought we might wo—" Cordelia didn't want her mother to know she had enlisted someone else to help her with the quilt.

"I'll see you after the funeral tomorrow." Gertie winked at her. "Go talk to your man."

Cordelia scrambled off the bed and bolted for the door. She threw it open the rest of the way as she charged past her mother. Her mother didn't follow. She didn't want an audience. She careened to a stop inside the screen door. She took a few calming breaths then stepped out onto the porch with her chin high.

Bernard sat on the edge of the swing with his hands in his lap. When he saw Cordelia, he rose and walked to her.

Gertie came out the door next. She cast a sideways glance at him, nodded, and strolled off down the stairs to the street.

His puzzled gaze watched Gertie for a few seconds, then he turned to Cordelia. "I'm sorry about your grandma. I know you really loved her a lot." He took her hands in his.

Cordelia relaxed at the warmth of his touch. She searched his face. She saw no hint of deception in his tone or his eyes. Her tension abated. She measured her words. "Where have you been?"

Bernard lowered his eyes. Cordelia's neck tightened.

Two women, dressed in their Sunday best, ascended the stairs to the porch. Each carried trays covered with paper bags. Both women glanced at Bernard holding Cordelia's hands. She slipped her hands from his and pressed her sweaty palms to her sides. She turned her attention back to Bernard and lifted a brow, waiting for an answer.

"I . . . I had to work yesterday. I'm sorry."

"On Sunday? What happened to going to church on Sunday?" Why would he tell her such a thing and expect her to believe him? If anyone missed church for a reason like work, it'd be her—not Mister Spiritually Mature.

He hung his head. "Please don't get mad—"

"Don't get mad about what?" Cordelia felt the color rise in her face. "Where were you?" As if she didn't know! If blood could heat in a person's veins and not kill them, hers had reached a rolling boil at this moment.

"I had to work on a car yesterday morning. JJ Jackson's mother needed work done on her car, but they wanted to go to

Philadelphia yesterday afternoon, therefore it had to be done in the morning."

Cordelia backed away. "Why didn't you just turn down the job, rather than miss church?"

"I couldn't afford to turn it down. I needed the money. My father's complaining I don't give enough to the household." Bernard pressed his lips as though restraining rising resentment.

Was he telling the truth? He knew that woman's name would set her off. He risked that much. Cordelia remembered why she was going to see him on Saturday, when the JJ scene sent her to the moon. "I . . . I was coming to see you Saturday to tell you about your father."

"What about my father?"

Cordelia bought a few seconds as she moved to the swing and sat down.

"Cordelia, what about my father?" Bernard sat beside her.

She hadn't thought about what telling him could do. What if it started a fight between Bernard and his father?

"Maybe I was mistaken."

"You came all the way to the garage on Saturday to tell me you were mistaken?"

"No! I came to tell you that I saw your fa—" she blurted out.

"You saw my father? That's impossible. He was working in the mine on Saturday."

Cordelia lowered her eyes. "That's why I said maybe I was mistaken."

Bernard tipped his head as though he were thinking. "Where do you think you saw him?"

She realized she'd also have to admit to the visit at the Strand on Saturday. Why hadn't she thought this through first?

"I . . . I didn't. I said I was mistaken."

Bernard started to protest. The screen door opened and Cordelia's mother stuck her head out. "I need you to help Mrs. Davidson set out the food she brought."

"I have to go. I'll see you after the funeral tomorrow." Cordelia took this providence to escape.

"I'm working extra shifts at the garage. I don't know when I'll see you."

Cordelia started to open the door, but stopped. "What time do you get off?"

"Not till about ten at night."

Cordelia knew her father would be upset if she went out that late.

"Cordelia, I need you in the kitchen, please," said her mother.

She looked back and forth. "I have to go."

Bernard caught the door. "I need to see you. We have to talk."

"I'll see you this weekend." She escaped inside, leaving him holding the screen door open.

She'd have to figure out how to tell him about his father without admitting how she knew. Or maybe she should forget the whole thing and let sleeping dogs lie, as Grammy used to say.

11

August 28, 1942

With all the many distractions after Grammy's death, the war in Europe, and the war with her mother, the lazy days of summer vacation flew by. Already it was the last Friday of August, and Cordelia had seen Bernard only in passing for several weeks. He spent the majority of his time at Stoney's or working with the church youth.

She plodded along the exposed cobblestones in the tar-pea gravel road down the center of Forest Court. She'd walked a half block down Olive Street as the oppressive August heat drenched her in sweat. She lifted the damp blouse away from her skin, remembering that her mother always insisted ladies glistened, while men perspired. Only horses sweat.

Day Hollow Manufacturing, the clothing factory, had won a contract for military uniforms. Almost every girl Cordelia knew had a sewing job for the summer. Some of them, like Gertie, had quit school to work full-time.

Cordelia strolled past the alley door and seated herself in the shade of the building. She set out the paper bag of peanut butter sandwiches and soda on the rough-hewn surface of an employee picnic table.

The lunch bell whistled high and long. Women streamed out of the double doors. Heat whooshed out of the building as the throng enveloped Cordelia. How much hotter was it inside? Gertie, carried along by the flow of traffic, popped out from the left side of the scattering group. She pulled a soaked handkerchief from her short, nappy hair and fanned herself with the loose edges. Her dark skin glistened with moisture.

"Girl, let me tell you, working in that sweltering place today should put the fear of God in all people," she said with a heavenward glance.

"Why?" Cordelia imagined some new horror, like the woman Gertie described who lost a finger to the pattern-cutting blade.

Gertie hitched her thumb over her shoulder. "Because it's hotter than Hades in there. That's what it's like to suffer hellfire and damnation. You should come get a job after you graduate. Misery loves company."

Cordelia tried to hold it in, but she burst out laughing at the comment. The idea was outrageous, but her brain latched onto it.

She scooped the peanut butter sandwiches out of the bag. The Food Rationing Program controlled everything she liked except peanut butter. She displayed her best grin as she slid the bottle of Coca-Cola from the lunch bag.

Gertie's eyes widened and she clapped her hands. "Oh my goodness! Where did you get that?" She snatched the small bottle from Cordelia and held the cool glass to her cheek.

"My dad had to go to Tobyhanna Army Depot yesterday. They have vending machines that sell to the soldiers. Can you imagine? They aren't rationing soda on the base! They say it's a morale builder."

"Well, it's building my morale," laughed Gertie.

Cordelia offered a bottle opener. "Easy with that. I shook the bag. We don't want to waste any."

Gertie pried the cap off the bottle, took a swig, and passed it to Cordelia.

Cordelia also took a long gulp and set it on the table. They unwrapped the waxed paper from their sandwiches.

Gertie bit into her sandwich. As she chewed she watched Cordelia intently. "I really appreciate the lunch. You know you don't have to do this."

"I know I don't, but you've been faithful at helping me work on my quilt, and you said you didn't have the extra money to buy lunch. That isn't right. We've got plenty of peanut butter, and the slices of bread are so fat I just slice through each with a sharp knife and turn one thick slice into two regulars. Technically, this is my one sandwich for lunch." Cordelia winked.

Gertie took another drink of Coca-Cola. "You're a good friend, Cordelia Grace. But I can't help noticing you're a little long in the jaw."

Cordelia chewed a bite of sandwich and watched a drop of condensation slide down the cool soda bottle. "Do you believe God had anything to do with our meeting?"

Gertie stopped chewing. "What kind of question is that? Is that why you look down?"

She swallowed hard and peered at Gertie. "I feel like I'm losing everything and nothing can stop it. I've lost Grammy. And I very seldom see Bernard."

Gertie waved the hand that held the remaining piece of sandwich. "What's going on with him? You two used to be inseparable."

"I think my father is finding things to make me busy to keep us apart. He's upset. Dad says Bernard is hanging around with some boys who aren't very spiritual."

Gertie slapped the table. "Well, that's the last straw! 'Not very spiritual' means they need to be banished from this world."

Cordelia's eyes widened. She sat back from the table. "Are you serious?"

Gertie burst out laughing. "Of course not. You looked somber, so I thought I'd play along."

Cordelia mumbled. "I don't feel very spiritual either."

"I've noticed when we're working on the quilt, you rarely offer a prayer."

"I don't feel anything." Cordelia plopped an elbow on the table and stuck her chin on her raised hand. "Especially since Grammy died. What's the use? I loved Grammy very much and I prayed really hard she'd be with me for a long time, even after I got married. What good did it do? She died anyhow."

"I bet people who've been praying for the war to end, or their men to be safe, are having a tough time with praying too. It's just part of having faith that God knows better."

"I've seen a lot of people changing lately." Even her times spent with Bernard were getting few and far between.

Gertie nodded. "People's attitudes *have* changed about everything because of this war. Just look at this place. Two years ago coloreds would never have been able to get a job here. The Italian and Chinese immigrants held on to these jobs forever and the ILGWU favored them over us. But the war changed that. Now they're hiring every one of us they can get. Thirty-five cents an hour is a lot of money."

"What's ILGWU?"

"That's the International Ladies Garment Workers Union. We all had to join. Don't get me wrong. There are a few mean ones. Segregation is alive and well down South and some of it does seem to drift here, but for the most part the union looks out for us."

"They look out for you? When you came outside it was a hundred degrees in there."

"And that's with ten industrial fans going. I seriously think if those old Italian ladies weren't in there, they'd shut the fans off to save on the electricity."

Cordelia shook her head. Maybe she ought to rethink this job thing. "It looks like it's really hard work."

"I caught onto the job real fast. I'm sewing pant legs. I could make piece rate if they'd let me. But those little old ladies are a mess. One of them keeps yelling at me in her broken accent, 'You breaka the rate. You breaka the rate.' They don't want me sewing faster than they do, because if I start making too much money on piecework, the foreman will lower the rate and they'll have to produce more to get the same amount of pay they get now."

"How fast can you sew?" Cordelia only knew how to sew on her mother's Singer, which had a treadle that didn't go any faster than she could pump her feet.

Gertie smiled. "You've never been in a sewing factory?"

Cordelia shook her head.

"These are electric machines. They sew twenty times faster than your home machine. Yesterday another one of the new girls had an accident. She says she wasn't paying attention and sewed her finger, jammed the machine, and then bled all over the pants she was waisting. That sure made for excitement."

Cordelia's eyes widened. She hadn't considered injury as part of a seamstress job.

"But if you ask me, I think the shop steward Vinnie had something to do with it," said Gertie.

"Why would you think that? I thought you said the union looked out for you?"

"I saw him hightailing it out of her area right when she started screaming. No one else seemed to notice. When I asked her about it, she denied it and turned all ashy gray."

"But what could he gain by hurting her?" At seventeen, and being a preacher's kid, she had never been involved with anything more nefarious than kids hiding the pew Bibles before service or the bullying of the Wilson kids.

"I don't know, but she's been real quiet and withdrawn today. I'm going to find out what's what."

"If she got hurt because of something going on, then it's dangerous, and maybe you should let it go. Or maybe you shouldn't be working there at all."

Gertie snickered. "I'm not leaving a good paying job just because of Mob activity." She shook her head. "There's something going on. I haven't quite figured out what it is. It seems like too much work comes and goes, and I'm not seeing how it's getting done. We don't have a night shift."

Cordelia searched Gertie's face, looking for fear. None showed. "Are you sure it's safe to work here?"

Women trickled back into the building.

Gertie laughed. "I have to get back. Are you coming to Courthouse Square this evening?"

"Sure. See you there." Cordelia noticed Gertie never answered the question. She wondered what trouble Gertie could get into now.

Gertie finished her last bite, used her two fingers to wipe the corners of her mouth, and balled the waxed paper before shoving it in the bag. "I've got someone for you to meet."

"Who? What are you doing?" The last time Gertie had a friend for her to meet it wound up being a loan shark enforcer for the Mob. Her constant string of boyfriends left something to be desired. Cordelia took one last gulp of Coke and handed the rest to Gertie, who finished the bottle and slid it into the paper bag as she rose from the bench.

"Never you mind. Here comes your sweetie." Gertie pointed down the Court.

Cordelia watched Bernard and several other young men horsing around and bouncing basketballs. She wondered how boys could expend such energy in this sweltering noonday heat. She wiped the back of her hand across her forehead and rose from the seat. She hung back inside the building's shadow, out of the scorching sun.

Bernard spotted her and waved. He jogged over and gave her a peck on the cheek. "Hey, girl. What you doing down here?" He eyed the building with the Hiring NOW! sign plastered on the side.

Having his breath that close to her neck made her shiver. She shook it off and answered his question with her own. "What are you doing off work?" Another example of a time he could be with her, but wasn't.

"The engine parts we were waiting on haven't come yet. The distributors fill the military orders first and we get left-overs." He raised an eyebrow. "Stoney gave me the afternoon off. I went by the church playground and grabbed the boys for a game of b-ball at the school court." Bernard eyed her. "As I asked . . . what are you doing down here?" By the look on his face, he'd assumed the worst.

"How about I was just walking by? What's the problem?" High time people started treating her like an adult. That included Bernard, especially since he chose to be absent from her life lately.

Relief crossed his face, and he nodded. "I thought you might be looking for a job."

"And the problem with that would be?" She put both hands to her hips.

"Hey, babe, listen, I don't want to fight." He gave a slight jerk of his head toward the roughhousing around him.

Cordelia reined in her attitude. "I had lunch with Gertie Truitt. She works here now."

Bernard grimaced. "She's a nice girl, a tad fast, but nice. I play ball with her older brother once in a while." One of the boys bumped into him holding a ball. Bernard sidestepped, palmed the ball, and took it with him. He dribbled a circle around the boy. The others burst into laughter with jokes about Bernard's speed.

Cordelia enjoyed watching Bernard have fun with the kids. Her anger abated. She was happy that her father had given him responsibility and hoped he'd be able to keep the job. He ribbed the kids a minute and turned back to Cordelia.

She tipped her head. Sweat plastered her single pigtail to her collarbone. She flipped it away nonchalantly. "Gertie invited me to Courthouse Square this evening. Want to come with me?"

"That's probably not the best place to hang out. Several rough people have been known to gather there. I hear talk."

"Well, I'm going." Cordelia's independence decided to show, though Bernard was usually right about being cautious.

Bernard tousled the hair of the cute redheaded kid with a mass of freckles across his nose. "I have to finish with the kids and then run home. I'd rather you didn't go. But I'll meet you there, if only to keep you out of trouble."

12

The sun hung low in the sultry evening sky above Courthouse Square. Cordelia wore her cutest pale blue pleated skirt and matching short-sleeved blouse with a bold blue and gold scarf tied at her neck. She'd rather have worn the new slim trousers she had sewed herself. But her father frowned on women wearing pants. He'd been at home when she left. There was no getting around it.

She walked across the grass to the Soldiers Monument, where at least a dozen teens had gathered around the base or were sitting on the step. A quick scan and she spotted Gertie. She leaned against some guy on the monument landing as he relaxed against one of the pillars. Cordelia waved.

Gertie returned the wave and nudged the guy to his feet. "Hey, girl! Glad to see you made it. I want to introduce you to Robert Burns. He's my new beau." She pulled the reluctant guy forward.

Cordelia extended her hand. "Glad to meet you, Robert. I don't know you from the neighborhood or church. Where do you come from?" She sized him up. His short wiry hair was slicked back on the sides with oily pomade. The top sported loose curls. He looked too mature to be a teen, with his pressed slacks, starched dress shirt, and shiny watch. His twenties?

"He's from New York City." Gertie stepped in. "He's part of the new production team taking a tour of our plant." She gestured at the small group of men standing several feet away.

Robert appeared to hush her, but Gertie paid him no mind. "He's invited me to visit him in the city," she added.

Now Robert looked visibly upset. Cordelia guessed if he hadn't had a cocoa complexion she'd have been able to see his cheeks get red.

Bernard walked along Spruce Street toward the group. "Well, Robert, I hope you take care of Gertie when she comes to the city. I've heard it's pretty hectic down there."

Robert stammered an answer Cordelia couldn't decipher. Bernard strolled near and slipped an arm around her waist. She looked at him and smiled.

"Who is this?" Bernard watched Robert as though he were jealous of the fellow's close proximity to her.

Cordelia giggled. Good to know he cared. "This is Gertie's new friend, Robert."

Bernard extended his hand. Robert's group of friends erupted in laughter and horseplay. One of the men side-stepped a random blow from one of the group and backed into Cordelia, throwing her off balance. She plopped to the grass with a squeak of surprise.

"Hey!" yelled Bernard as he shoved back on the guy. "Watch what you're doing."

He bent over to help her just as the offender pushed back. Bernard stumbled. He spun around and came out with fists swinging.

Cordelia scrambled out of the way. "Stop! What is wrong with you two?"

Two of Bernard's friends hopped down off the monument and ran to join the altercation. Neither asked what had happened. They just jumped into the fight, punching people they didn't know. Cordelia tried to get Bernard to stop. She was shoved back, and Gertie caught her as she careened from the melee.

"Do something," Cordelia yelled at Gertie.

Gertie grimaced. "I'm not getting in there." She looked down Spruce Street. "But they sure will." She pointed at the three police officers running toward them.

Cordelia sat on the long wooden bench in the police station behind the municipal building. How had this happened? The police had called her father to come and get her. She hadn't been arrested, but she'd been hauled into the station with the rest of the group. Their parents were notified of the disturbing the peace charge against the rowdy troublemakers.

She tapped her foot on the linoleum floor. What was she going to say?

"Cordelia," said her father.

She shrank into the latticework on the back of the bench and peeked from under her lashes. "Hi, Daddy. I'm sorry you had to come down here. I swear I wasn't in any trouble."

Her mother stood beside her father, looking more disgusted than he did. "I've had enough of these shenanigans, young lady. You're grounded for a month."

"But, Mom, I didn't do anything," pleaded Cordelia.

"The fact that you were in the same place where these hoodlums rioted is bad enough," said her father. "It's a good thing you aren't being charged with anything." He snatched her to her feet and directed her to the door. Her mother followed behind.

"Wait! I have to see what they did with Bernard." She tried to duck back.

"Bernard? Is he involved in this?" Her father's face froze in a scowl.

Cordelia nodded. "He was defending me—"

"Defending you?" Her father paced in front of her. "Am I to understand you were involved in this?"

"Well, yes, er, uh, no! It was a misunderstanding."

Her father grabbed her by the arm again. "Yes, there has been a misunderstanding, and it's mine. Bernard was supposed to keep you safe from situations like this, not get you into them."

She struggled to keep her dignity as her father hauled her out of the police station by the elbow. "It wasn't Bernard's fault. It was mine." She wiggled to get free but he held her in a vise-like grip.

He frowned at her. "Don't be ridiculous. You're a girl. I blame this on Bernard. He should have known better."

Cordelia saw her mother's expression change with his comment, but Mom held her tongue.

She jerked loose from her father. "I'm not leaving without him. This is NOT his fault."

"You will get in the automobile right now, young lady, or face the punishment."

Cordelia pressed her fists into her waist. Defiance masked her fear of disobedience. "I'm not leaving."

"I'll give you to the count of five and then you're on punishment until the end of October. One . . . two . . ."

Cordelia figured she could handle a two-month punishment, if she could get to where Bernard was at the moment.

"Cordelia, don't be silly. Come along," said her mother.

"Five! That's it. Let's go. Now!"

Cordelia hung back. She was in too deep now to relent. "No, I'm staying."

"November," said her father.

"Emanuel," said her mother. "Don't you think this has gone too—"

Her father shot a glance at her mother.

Cordelia refused to move.

"December," said her father. "And I'm beginning to realize just how bad an influence Bernard is on you. You are not to see him again."

Cordelia opened her mouth to protest. Her mother signaled with her fingers to zip her lip. She'd pushed her father too far.

13

December 15, 1942

The strains of Bing Crosby singing "White Christmas" drifted in from the living room.

"Listen, either you're going to blame God for all the things you think are happening to ruin your life, or you're going to get on your knees and let God help you get through it," said Gertie. She lock-stitched a triangle into place.

Cordelia gnawed on her bottom lip. "He hates me. This is punishment because I didn't have enough faith to believe things could change if I prayed."

She still wasn't convinced prayer helped. After all, she'd screamed out in prayer when Grammy died, and it didn't make a difference. Didn't God know Grammy was her whole world? She was determined to finish this quilt for Grammy's sake. It would have pleased her to know that her granddaughter finished the project in honor of her.

"Oh, brother. Do you really think God . . ." Gertie spread her hands above her head, "the Creator of the Universe, *didn't* know you were going to smart-mouth your father and get grounded until the end of time?"

"You're starting to sound like Grammy again."

Gertie put her hand on Cordelia's shoulder. "Honey, God is no respecter of persons. He looks at every one of us the same. All you need is a mustard seed worth of faith to build on."

Cordelia stuck her needle into the pincushion and rested her head in her hand. "My life is ruined. Do you realize it's almost Christmas and I haven't spent more than five minutes at a time with Bernard since September?"

Gertie snickered. "I guess your Grammy was right, nothing spoils a duck but its bill."

"I couldn't help myself. I was worried about Bernard, and my father wouldn't give me a chance to explain."

"But Bernard didn't get charged with anything. If you'd left well enough alone, everything would have been fine." Gertie folded another triangle. "I'm going to pray that you find the sense the good Lord gave you."

Cordelia shook her head. "It still wouldn't have been fine. Dad met with the church Board, and I don't know if it was his idea or theirs, but Bernard lost his position with the youth."

"I wondered why I haven't seen him around church much anymore."

"He hasn't been coming regularly since that happened. And being on punishment, I can't get to his house to find out what's going on." Cordelia was counting the days until her torture ended. She had to get through Christmas. She missed Bernard with an ache that made her chest hurt. For a while she blamed him. Yes, illogical, since she was the grounded person. But it was easier to blame him than her own impetuousness.

The few times she saw him in passing, invariably one parent or the other cut short the encounter. They effectively banished him from her life.

"Can't you call him on the telephone?" Gertie plucked another square and started folding.

Cordelia cocked her head. "Are you kidding me? One of the parent police is usually home. If they aren't, someone on the party line would tell. Then I'd be dead all over again."

"Hasn't he tried to get in touch with you?" Gertie grabbed another square to fold.

"No, I think he tried to wave last Sunday, but Mom hustled me out of the sanctuary. Why?"

"I'm just wondering if he's messin' with someone else. It's been quite a few months, and I would've expected him sneaking around to see you."

Bile rose in her throat. Cordelia gulped to push away the sensation of nausea.

———

Bernard stood in front of the grimy auto shop window, hands shoved in his pockets, staring out at the falling snow.

Stoney walked up behind him. "Listen, I'm sorry I busted your chops about Cordelia."

"That's okay. I was a real dope to think her father would understand." It didn't help any that his own father kept rubbing it in. Every night at dinner, then again every morning at breakfast. Nothing but taunts about the uppity girl who dumped him. They had taken a toll.

"When I came to the police station to get you that night, they assured me it wasn't your fault. Didn't they clear it up with her father?"

"I guess not. She got punished because of me." Bernard kicked at a wooden box of cast-off automobile parts. He hadn't seen Cordelia in four months. "By the way, I don't remember if I ever thanked you for coming to sign me out. My father refused. He said I got myself into trouble and I could get myself out."

Stoney nodded. "You're welcome. But with your father that's no front-page news. Did you go see her father?"

"He wouldn't listen to reason. He called me a hoodlum and informed me that my services were no longer needed with the kids." He never thought defending the girl he loved could put him on the wrong side of her father. But Cordelia's father hadn't been sympathetic to his part in the park altercation.

"That's a bit harsh. But maybe it all happened for the good. Could be time to find a new woman," said Stoney, wiping his hands on the greasy rag from his back pocket.

Bernard wheeled to face him. "You think losing Cordelia is a good thing?" This was another voice added to those of the guys who told him to move on and find another woman. Many girls, including JJ Jackson, cornered him at every opportunity. He had to admit a couple of gals were mighty fine and ripe for the picking, but his heart wasn't in it.

Stoney shrugged his shoulders but remained silent.

Bernard snatched his coat from the hook by the front door. He had no one who understood his pain and frustration.

He hunched his shoulders, pulling his collar up around his ears to ward off the icy wind. Silent snowflakes swirled around him, blanketing the Court. The new-fallen layer of snow looked fresh and clean, unlike the reality of his situation. The world hated him, and sometimes he thought God hated him too.

It seemed quite long ago. *I'm a fool.* Mom had been right all along, including about the church. They'd thrown him away when they no longer had a use for him. He stopped going to church regularly because people snickered and talked about him behind his back. Conversations stopped when he came near.

He needed Cordelia.

But in a moment of desperation and weakness he had decided to show them all!

He trudged up the Court and reached for the latch on his gate.

Uncle Sam's posters hung along the length of the fence. "We need you in the Army."

14

December 31,1942

Cordelia sat in Grammy's rocker with her head resting against the high back and her eyes closed. She rocked in tandem with the ticking of her alarm clock and the beat of the music drifting under her bedroom door. This was the first New Year's Eve she hadn't joined the party. She could hear the adults moving down the hall and out onto the porch. Pots and pans, the prerequisite form of ushering in the New Year, clanked together, drowning out the murmuring of the crowd. Thoughts of tomorrow commanded her attention. The stroke of midnight, mere seconds away, and the punishment ended. She would be able to see Bernard.

January 1, 1943

Cordelia scuffed along the Court, disrupting the fresh-fallen snow with the tip of her boots. The morning sun sat low in the eastern sky. It strained to provide warmth on a frigid day, while anticipation washed over her in growing waves warming her heart.

Her parents were still sleeping after last night's revelry. She tiptoed out the door so as not to wake them. Technically, she wasn't disobeying any rules. Her father hadn't forbidden her to see Bernard. But he had declared that Bernard was no longer part of the ministry team at church.

She knew that was her father's pastoral language for "he's not an adequate role model." But she refused to listen. Frosty breath billowed out of her mouth as she raced away from the negative thoughts projected by her father.

The gate. She focused her gaze on the worn wooden structure. Would Bernard suddenly appear and wrap her in his arms? Her heartbeat pounded on the walls of her chest.

She reached for the handle and hesitated. What if Bernard's father answered the door? She'd heard about him being a mean drunk and a brawler. He frightened her. Cordelia's knees shook as she climbed the porch steps. Her hands trembled. She should wait for Bernard to come to her house. But what if her father had told him to stay away? She could look for him at Stoney's tomorrow. She turned to leave.

The front door swung open. "Cordelia, is that you all hidden in that bundle of coat?"

Cordelia flinched. "Yes, ma'am. It's me." She stammered, "I came to see Bernard."

Anna Howard wiped her hands on her apron and motioned Cordelia in. "Come in, child, before you catch your death."

His mother looked pleasant enough. Maybe she didn't know what had transpired with Bernard and the church. She could imagine him withholding information to avoid dampening his mother's return to faith. The kitchen smelled like peaches. The heat from the stove pressed in like hands around her face. She pushed back the scarf from her head and unfastened the

113

buttons on her coat, all the while glancing around for Bernard—
or his father. The two thoughts pulled opposite emotions from
her.

Anna grabbed two potholders and opened the oven to
retrieve a pie. "Bernard loves peaches. I made his favorite for
the first day of the new year."

"Is he home?" Cordelia hadn't moved from the closed door.
Close enough to feel safe for a fast getaway, but far enough
inside to look hospitable.

"Bernard went to the coal breaker with his father to gather
scraps."

Cordelia's fingers curled around the door handle. Were
forces in the world conspiring to keep them apart? "I can come
back later."

"No, child, stay," said Anna as she motioned to her left.
"Go on in the living room and have a seat. They'll be back any
minute."

Cordelia cringed. Why did adults continue to call her
child? She'd graduate high school in seven months, and that
was adulthood. She moved toward the open doorway. A mul-
ticolored Pinecone Quilt was draped over the back of the
couch. Her uneasiness dissolved. She hurried to the couch to
touch the pattern. A strange sensation settled in her stomach.
Someone else understood.

"I hear them coming now," announced Anna.

Cordelia jerked her hand from the quilt. Manners dictated
she should ask before touching someone else's things.

Anna smiled. "It's all right, child."

"Was this made for you? I have one my Grammy was making for me, but she died before it was done. I'm finishing it
myself." Cordelia hung her head.

Anna joined Cordelia on the couch. She lowered her voice
to almost a whisper. "I was making this for my baby girls."

"Girls? I thought Bernard was an only child."

"My girls are in heaven—"

The front door banged open. Anna flinched. She hurried from the couch to the kitchen. "Charles, is Bernard right behind you? His Cordelia is here to visit."

How fragile Anna's voice became when she spoke to her husband. Cordelia could sense the fear. How could a person live like that?

"He's shoveling the coal into the cellar," boomed the scratchy voice.

Cordelia hopped from the couch as though she had been stung. Even his voice made her nervous. She scooted up behind Anna and peered into the kitchen. Anna turned and looked at her. She flicked an unconvincing smile. No way out except past him. She'd never been this close to Bernard's father before.

Charles glared at her. "I thought you high-and-mighty Graces had washed your hands of my son."

Cordelia followed Anna into the kitchen but kept the table and chairs as a comfort barrier.

"Leave the child alone. She had nothing to do with her father's decisions." Anna turned to her. "Did you, child?"

For once Cordelia didn't mind being called a child. She hoped he wouldn't think it right to hit someone else's child. Her words stuck in her dry throat. She shook her head.

Charles moved around the table.

Cordelia bypassed Anna and hurried to the door. "I have to go now."

She closed the door and raced down the steps, glancing behind her to see if the door stayed closed. She ran headlong into an unmovable object. Cordelia screamed. Arms wrapped around her. Bernard's lips pressed against hers. She whimpered and wrapped her arms around his neck, returning the kiss until neither of them could breathe.

Her hands moved to caress his cold cheeks. "I missed you so much. You didn't come to find me and I tried to talk to you in church, but they—"

"Shhh," said Bernard. He pulled off a glove and gently touched her face with the back of his fingers. "It's all right. Gertie told me about your punishment. I didn't want to make it worse by getting you in more trouble."

"It wasn't your fault in the first place. You were trying to protect me."

"I told your father I handled it badly, and for that I was sorry. But I wasn't sorry that I defended you."

Cordelia tightened her grip around his neck and kissed him. She never wanted to be away from him again. Tears rolled down her cheeks.

Bernard smiled. "What are you crying about?"

"I love you. I don't care what my father says, I'm going to marry you when I graduate in June."

There was a loosening of his arms. Bernard lowered his head.

Cordelia felt a rush of adrenaline pulse through her chest. She was afraid to speak.

She searched his face. "What's the matter?" A nervous laugh choked its way from her throat. "You act like . . . like you don't . . ." she couldn't even contemplate the thought, "love me anymore."

Bernard looked up for a second. His mouth opened but then it closed.

"Bernard!" Her heart pounded so hard it made her wobble.

"I didn't do it on purpose."

"What have you done?" Cordelia released his neck and stumbled against the steps. Bernard caught her before she fell and pulled her back into his arms.

She thrust his hands away. "Answer me!" Her mind went to JJ Jackson or a whole host of other beautiful, available girls and visualized scenes she didn't want to contemplate.

"I signed up for the Army."

Her brain couldn't process, didn't want to process, what he'd just said. Was he speaking a foreign language?

Bernard looked into her eyes.

Her lip trembled. "No, this is a mistake. Take it back. Tell them you didn't mean to—"

He shook his head. "I can't take it back. I got my letter yesterday."

"What letter?"

"My number came up in the lottery. I've been drafted."

"But they can't do that. You aren't eighteen yet."

"I lied on the application at the Selective Service Board."

Cordelia punched him in the arm. "Why did you do a stupid thing like that?"

"Because I was angry at everybody."

Cordelia lowered her voice. "Even me?"

"Especially you." Bernard turned away. "I felt deserted."

"But it wasn't my fault. Well, maybe some of it was. I got punished." She remembered her mouthy outburst at her parents. "We need to fix this. They can't take you because you aren't eighteen, and that settles it."

"I don't report until January twenty-second. I'll legally turn eighteen by then."

Cordelia's knees wobbled, and she sank to the snow-covered steps. How could this be happening? Did God hate her? What had she done to deserve all this pain?

Bernard knelt in front of her. "I love you with all my heart. Will you marry me before I go?"

Her hands refused to move. The breath caught in Cordelia's chest. "Yes, I will marry you." Tears rolled down her cheeks melting the fresh snowflakes. She threw her arms around him. She'd heard some men received exemptions for being married. They'd get married right away. Her mind ticked off the steps to solve their problem.

No one would take him from her without a fight.

15

January 18, 1943

You heard me," growled her father's voice. He restrained himself, but Cordelia could see the veins popping out on his forehead. "There will be no wedding!"

"I love him! The Army is going to take him away from me on Friday. Can't you see this is my last chance? You're ruining my life!" She stormed to the couch and threw herself on the end opposite her mother. Cordelia begged until she felt the heat radiating from her face, but neither relented.

"You can perform all you want, Sarah Bernhardt, but no daughter of mine will be a high school dropout," said her mother. Cordelia understood her defeat. Her mother's comparison of her to the dramatic actress meant her words were falling on deaf ears.

Cordelia furrowed her brows and dropped the drama. "What are you talking about? I wouldn't quit high school."

"Yes, you would," said her father. "You'd need to get a job to support yourself because you wouldn't be living in this house after defying me."

Her glare traveled in his direction. "You would throw me out of the house because I want to save Bernard from going to war?"

119

Her father set his jaw. "Yes." He turned away from her and looked to the ceiling. "I will do what I must to protect you from him."

She jumped to her feet. "I hate you, and I will never forgive you for ruining our lives."

Her mother touched Cordelia's arm. "Darling, you need to listen—"

Cordelia yanked her arm away. "I'm done listening to either of you. When I graduate you will never see me again." She stormed out.

"Cordelia—"

"Let her go," said her father. "She'll see we're right in the long run."

Cordelia darted into her bedroom and slammed the door with all the force she could muster. Why had this gone so horribly wrong? Yesterday at church she'd prayed with every ounce of strength she had.

God was a fraud. He hadn't answered anything.

Her quilt lay across Grammy's rocker. The pent-up rage boiled out. She screamed and snatched the quilt. Her hands wrapped themselves in the edges of the cloth as she tried to rip it apart. The material resisted. Tears welled up in her eyes. She lashed out and beat the material on the edge of the dresser. A brush, two combs, and numerous bobby pins flew everywhere.

Cordelia raged at the quilt. She slammed it into every piece of furniture in the room, until her arm grew tired and she couldn't lift it anymore.

She slid in a heap to the floor at the foot of her bed, the quilt still wrapped around her right hand. She rocked. Bernard was going to war and she couldn't save him. She refused to believe God loved her. He hated her like her parents did.

The quilt. What had she done? She panicked. Had she torn Grammy's creation? She turned it over in her hands.

Undamaged. The words *thank God* almost escaped her lips. She silenced them. Not thanks to God, but to Grammy, who'd sewn such a strong quilt.

She wrapped the quilt around her shoulders and continued to rock. "Grammy, what am I going to do? They're taking Bernard away. I may never see him again." Gertie had told her she was a little cuckoo talking out loud to her dead grandmother, but she found comfort in thinking Grammy watched over her.

She'd celebrated Bernard's eighteenth birthday last Friday. But the celebration wasn't the anticipated happy gathering. For Cordelia and his mom, the sobering reality intruded that Bernard would leave for the United States Army in one week. But the men slapped him on the back, wished him well, and told him to get a Nip for them. Bernard had a dazed expression Cordelia could identify with.

He could get shot, or worse, wind up dead, when months ago getting hit by a basketball or a car jack slipping were the worst-case scenarios. Her mind couldn't stop conjuring images of Bernard broken and bleeding. He gasped for air, whispering her name with his last breath.

Cordelia shuddered and squeezed her eyes shut.

She'd never forgive her parents.

Bernard laid his gear out on the bed. Trainees had specific instructions about how little they could bring. The Army was their new family, and it would provide. He loaded toiletries into a small leather case, then shoved it into the narrow duffle bag.

His father leaned against the doorjamb. Bernard continued shoving underwear and socks into the duffle. It was bad enough that Cordelia and his mother ranted about him leaving. He wasn't in the mood to hear his father call his move stupid.

"Boy, I want to talk to you before you leave."

Here it comes. Bernard kept packing. The loathing for this man would probably never abate, even with time apart. "Yes, sir, what can I do for you?"

Charles shoved his hands into his pockets as though he couldn't get out what he wanted to say. "I know we've never been close—"

"Oh, we've been plenty close many a time. I remember all of them . . . sir."

"I'm sorry about that, boy."

Bernard turned to look at his father. For a second, he almost believed him. But he dismissed it as wishful thinking. "Is that what you wanted to tell me . . . sir?" He turned back to packing.

"No, that wasn't it at all." His father slid his hands from his pockets and stood up straight. "I wanted to say I'm proud of you, boy. You've turned into a right fine man. I hope you come home safe."

Bernard turned. His father was gone. Bernard's shoulders slumped. For the record, his stupid Army move had created the most memorable moment of his life. His father had never said he was proud of him.

Bernard wanted to follow after him and say thanks, but that second of elation passed. The pain of all the lost years rolled in like a storm cloud.

He'd never turn out like his father.

16

January 22, 1943

Cordelia stood in the waiting area outside the Greyhound Bus station on Adams Avenue. Bernard was inside with his mother and father. She wanted Bernard's mother to have her own time to say good-bye. Besides, Cordelia wanted to be at the last place she would see him before he left. Remember the last place she would be able to touch him.

The biting January winds stormed along the narrow strip where the buses were parked diagonally at the curb. She pulled her coat tighter. Maybe it'd be better to wait inside. Then again, someone at the restaurant counter might tell her parents they saw her. She had skipped the last two periods of school to see Bernard off. Her father would have a conniption fit.

She hunched into her coat and shivered. An arm slid around her shoulders. Bernard. He swung around and touched his lips to hers. Her chest tingled as she drew a long breath and inhaled his Old Spice aftershave scent. How long could she hold it? If she let it out, she'd ruin the moment. Her arms wound around his neck. She wanted to freeze this moment in time for eternity.

Bernard held her at arm's length and grinned. "Girl, if you'd been kissing me like this all along, I might not have joined the Army."

Cordelia blushed and lowered her arms. "I always thought there'd be time and we could take it slow. But now . . ." She didn't want him to see her desperation.

"Smile, baby doll." He put his fingers under her chin and lifted it.

"Stop being a fathead. How can you be so cavalier? You might not come—" The word strangled her throat.

"*Home.* Is that the word you're looking for?" Bernard wrapped his arms about her waist and spun her around.

She squirmed out of his grip. "Stop. I'm serious. I love you, and I want to be your wife."

Bernard grinned. "That's what I was waiting to hear." He held her hand and dropped to one knee.

Cordelia felt the tears welling in her eyes. She hoped it made them sparkle rather than look bloodshot.

"Will you marry me the day I come home?"

"Yes, yes, and twenty times more, yes!" cried Cordelia.

Bernard slipped a tiny gold band with a diamond chip onto her ring finger. He rose and wrapped her in his arms again.

They kissed until the loudspeaker broke the spell. "Bus now boarding for Fort Dix, New Jersey, on platform number 2."

Bernard broke away. "That's me, baby doll. Can't keep Uncle Sam waiting." He turned her loose and bolted to the line of young men on the same journey.

Cordelia clutched at thin air.

He sat in a window seat, waving out at her. She swallowed a strangled cry. She wanted to scream, claw at the bus, anything but wave good-bye.

Bernard pushed the window open. "I'll write as soon as I can."

The bus backed out and pulled forward onto Adams Avenue.

Cordelia ran along the walkway to the end of the lot, waving and crying the whole way. "I love you," she said knowing he could no longer hear her. Her life slipped through her hands.

Gone. He was gone.

Bernard craned his neck until he could no longer see Cordelia. He settled back into the seat, swallowed hard, and used his sleeve to brush away free-flowing tears. He couldn't let her see him cry. It wouldn't have helped the situation. This was hard enough.

What was he thinking when he signed up? What a stupid move. Granted, he would've had to sign up anyhow on his birthday. Who knows, he may have missed the lottery and not been chosen.

He watched the streets roll by. Who was he kidding? He couldn't avoid the draft for the whole war. His number would have come up sooner or later. The revelation soothed his battered conscience. An Italian kid from Dunmore sat across the aisle. Bernard recognized him from the basketball league. The guy smiled and nodded. Bernard returned the nod.

"I'm Domenic Carlone." He stood and held out his hand. "I remember you from the basketball court."

Bernard shook his hand. "Bernard Howard. Yeah, I thought I recognized you. I'd ask where you're going, but I think we're all going to the same place." Bernard slid over to share his seat.

Domenic nodded and sat beside him. "Did you join or get drafted?"

"Both. I signed up early as though I was already eighteen, but by the time the notice date came, my birthday had come."

Domenic tapped on the armrest. "I gotta admit, I'm kinda nervous. I don't know anyone that's gone."

"Me, either," said Bernard. "I don't know what we're in for."

"Well, whatever it is, we'll do it together and get to make our country proud against those Nips."

It struck Bernard for the first time he might engage in battle with people who resembled his friends at the garden nursery. Why hadn't that occurred to him before?

Domenic's eyes were wide as he leaned in to whisper, "Have you ever shot a gun before?"

Bernard stared out the window. "No, and I guess I didn't think about having to kill other people either."

"Don't tell anybody, but I don't want to kill people and I don't know how to shoot a gun."

"I hope we get good training so we know what we're doing," said Bernard. He searched under his seat for the bag of snacks his mom had packed.

"They say infantry training is the best."

Bernard found the paper sack, looked inside, and held it out. "Want an apple?"

Domenic reached in the bag and helped himself to a shiny red Macintosh. They munched on the crispy treats. With their stomachs full, the droning wheels soon lulled them to sleep.

Several hours later, the bus pulled into the station at Fort Dix, New Jersey. The sudden silence woke both young men. Bernard stretched and yawned. He nodded to the other young men filing down the aisle to the exit.

Numerous buses littered the drop-off point. Young men of all shapes and sizes milled about as they gathered luggage and duffle bags.

"I guess we're in the Army now," joked Bernard.

Domenic stood and stretched his legs. "Home sweet home for at least the duration of the war."

Bernard hadn't thought about that either. The war could last a lot of years.

They laughed together as they exited the bus and joined the crowd. Two dark green buses waited in the lot. A uniformed solder stood equidistant between them.

"Inductees front and center," he repeated until the Greyhound had emptied.

All the young men lined up in front of him. The sergeant looked at Domenic and Bernard approaching him. He pointed at Domenic. "Mount the bus over there." He pointed to the bus to the right.

Bernard followed Domenic.

"Hey, boy!" The sergeant yelled at Bernard.

Bernard turned. Great. He wondered if his father had told this man to annoy him with the one word that set his teeth on edge. "Yes, sir." Bernard turned to face him.

"Don't call me sir, boy, I work for a living. Call me Drill Sergeant."

"Yes, Drill Sergeant." Bernard stood still. What else could he do?

The sergeant pointed to the bus on his left. "You get in that bus."

Bernard looked across at Domenic, who stopped to observe. Domenic waved. Bernard waved back and mounted the steps to the other bus. He looked up the aisle. All the young men on this bus were Negroes. He took an empty seat toward the middle and looked out the window at the bus across the way. Domenic looked out a window at him, too. All the men in Domenic's bus appeared to be white.

A tall, lanky, dark-skinned guy with close-cropped hair ambled up the aisle and sat next to Bernard. "Howdy," he said as he stuffed his long legs into the small space under the seat in front of him.

Bernard absently answered but continued looking out the window.

"I'm Luther Higgins. What would you be called?" asked the recruit.

"Excuse me?" said Bernard, diverting his gaze from the window. "I'm sorry. I'm Bernard Howard. Do you know what's going on?"

"What do you mean?"

"Why are those guys over there, and we're over here?"

Luther squinted out the window. "You mean those white boys over there?"

"Yes, one of the guys I came with is in that bus."

"You go around with white boys?"

Bernard set his chin. In Scranton, there was never any overt prejudice among ethnicities. "Yeah, what's the problem?"

Luther grinned and slouched into the seat. "Well, don't that beat all."

"You didn't answer me."

"Man, this is the United States Army. Us Negroes are segregated from the white boys."

17

March 2, 1943

Cordelia read Bernard's letters again as she rocked. The packet of three letters had arrived yesterday. She memorized the words, his handwriting, and the feel of the onionskin paper. She touched the stamps on the envelopes, anything to keep her closer to her love. Her heart ached.

While she had suffered through her months of punishment, at least she'd been able to sneak a peek at Bernard. She'd snuck over to Stoney's Garage for a glimpse of him, and Stoney had spotted her outside between the oil drums. He smiled, but she blushed and ran away. What she wouldn't give for the opportunity to see Bernard now, if only for a few seconds.

Gertie tromped into her bedroom.

"I'm getting tired of snow. Can we do some kind of sun dance to prompt spring?" Gertie pulled off her scarf, gloves, and hat, then worked at the buttons on her coat.

"Well, I have a day off from school, and your factory is closed because of the nasty weather. We can spend the day together."

"A snow day made for fun when I was in school, but I'm losing a day's pay." Gertie pushed the unfinished quilt to the end of the bed and sat on the hassock. She peeled off her outer layer of damp socks. "I left my boots on the mat at the front door. I didn't want your ma to get mad if I wet her floors."

"Who cares?" Cordelia gently refolded the letter and stuck it back in its envelope.

"Why are you angry at her?"

"You're shinin' me, right? What do I have to be mad about?" She held out the letters. "I wouldn't be reading letters from the man I love, who's on a ship somewhere in the South Pacific, if it weren't for them. I hate them!"

"Cordelia Grace, that is a very mean thing to say about your parents. They only did what they thought right."

"They thought not letting me marry Bernard to help him get an exemption would be right? He could die in some foreign country and I'd never lay eyes on him again. Well, I wish they'd die!"

Gertie stopped fiddling with her socks. "You don't really mean it, do you?"

Cordelia set her jaw, hugged the letters, and rocked the chair harder.

"Cordelia, we have to go out," Betty called from the hall.

She continued to rock and ignored her mother.

"Your mom is talking to you." Gertie fingered the last worked row of the quilt.

Cordelia glanced at her, refusing to answer.

"Cordelia." The door pushed open. Her mom stuck her head in. "We have to go to Lake Scranton."

Gertie puckered her lips. "In this snowstorm? Everything is closed."

Betty nodded in agreement. "We wouldn't go, but the man is dying and he wants a preacher before he meets his Maker. Emanuel's the only one available in the group." She looked at Cordelia. "We won't be late for dinner."

Cordelia never responded. She couldn't trust the words that would come out of her mouth. She understood part of the fault rested on Bernard for signing up early. He should have waited until they could discuss it. But he wasn't close enough to bear her wrath.

Her mother ignored the slight, smiled at Gertie, and closed the door.

"I know you're hurt, but acting like a spoiled brat is not helping the situation." Gertie snatched the quilt and proceeded to fold it.

"I'll get over it, but right now it's too raw. Every time I think I'm coming to terms with it, I reread a letter from Bernard instead of hear his voice. It makes me angry again."

"What's the deal with staying cooped up in this bedroom? This is depressing." Gertie laid the folded quilt along the end of the bed, smoothing it with her hands.

Cordelia rocked. "I don't want to be in the living room where I'd need to converse with them. My present attitude would get me punished again. I'm not sure how much more I can take being treated like a child."

Gertie smiled. "Then stop acting like one. Have they tried to talk to you?"

Cordelia set her jaw. Tears welled in her eyes and threatened to flood down her cheeks. She rocked harder, threatening to tip the chair over. Frustration simmered like a forgotten pot on the stove. Her parents hadn't entertained the thought she would have anything worth contributing to a conversation about age and the responsibilities of marriage. Her father said her opinion didn't count where Bernard was concerned. She was too young to understand. Her pot might boil dry and explode!

"If you're not willing to talk about them, let's talk about your quilt. It doesn't look like you've been doing much work on it," Gertie said.

Cordelia shrugged. She blinked and the drops slid down her cheeks. Helpless and confused, she hated her parents and loved them all at the same time. And Bernard . . . well, if the war didn't kill him, she'd beat him to death for volunteering too soon. "What good is it praying for my future? It hasn't done me much good up to now. I might never see Bernard again."

She realized during her punishment that she didn't believe prayers could affect her future. Grammy had talked her into praying for a few of those years, and nothing she'd prayed about ever turned out right. She'd continued working on the quilt because she loved Grammy and wanted to finish the project for her. Now even that seemed like a chore.

Gertie smiled. "Then it's Bernard you need to be praying for. Do you think your Grammy was just praying for you? She prayed about everyone who came into your life."

"You didn't even know my Grammy well. How can you say that?"

Gertie moved to Cordelia's bookshelf and picked up Grammy's Bible. "She wrote about what she prayed for you in here. Haven't you looked at her Bible?"

"I haven't had time. I've been busy." Cordelia barely understood all those thee's and thou's. She once turned to the Song of Solomon but it made her head hurt. She confined biblical studies to the Sunday school teacher's explanations.

Gertie shook her head and handed Cordelia the Bible. "Yeah, I'm sure being in this room for a couple months' punishment really consumed all your time."

Cordelia accepted the book. "When did you read her Bible?"

"When we brought her stuff in here the night of the wake. I was trying to tell you."

Cordelia sighed and sniffed back the rest of the tears. "Show me what you found now, please."

They sat for an hour cross-legged on the bed as Gertie showed Cordelia the letter Grammy had left for her, and the marked passages. It took a bit of explaining, but Cordelia didn't feel as helpless when they finished. Grammy's words, written as notes on the page margins, taught truth. Deep inside, a burden lifted.

"I'm assuming you don't read the Bible every day," said Gertie, as she gently closed the book.

"I can truthfully tell you, and only you, I haven't spent any time reading the Bible since I was about ten years old. Probably the only thing I remember is, 'Jesus wept.'"

Gertie ran her hand gently across the leather-embossed cover. "How? You're the pastor's kid. How do you *not* know the Bible?"

Cordelia shrugged. "Mom did the children's stories, like Adam and Eve, and Noah's Ark when I was little. Now that I'm a teenager, I guess they thought I was studying it in Sunday school. You know yourself, the Bible is not the hipster thing to do at seventeen if you want to go along with everyone else. And I don't care that you didn't care about being popular, but at the time, I wanted to be like everyone else in my crowd."

Gertie's teeth grated together, but then she shook her head. "Bernard. How is he?"

Cordelia brightened. "He seems to be good. He told me about some of the guys from New Jersey and down South. They came here to join to go to a Northern boot camp."

"Does it make a difference?"

"Bernard says there's less prejudice in New Jersey than there is in South Carolina."

Gertie moved to sit on the bed. "Prejudice in New Jersey? What's he talking about?"

Cordelia lowered her voice. "Whites and Negroes are segregated in the Army."

Gertie stared. "Why haven't we heard about this?"

"How much of the war have you paid attention to in the news?"

"Well . . . not much. Men killing each other and the politics don't interest me. When I get old, like in my thirties, then I'll be interested."

"Bernard says they have old guns from World War I for practice and half of them are falling apart. A few guys from the country are able to shoot the eyes out of a gnat."

"How is he handling being away from home?"

Cordelia shrugged her shoulders. "He says things are fine, other than him missing me terribly. His last letter is dated two weeks ago. He said their training was cut short and they're on a ship headed to the South Pacific. But he couldn't tell me where because he didn't know."

Pounding interrupted their chat.

"What is that?" asked Gertie.

The pounding intensified.

Cordelia hopped off the bed. "Someone's at the door."

Both girls hurried down the hall.

"Stop pounding before you break the glass," yelled Cordelia. "My dad will blow a fuse." She threw open the door.

Mr. Dempsey, a church elder, who was bundled against the cold, huffed and puffed, covered in snowflakes. "There's been an accident."

18

Bernard disembarked with the first crew from the 486th Port Battalion transport ship in Noumea, New Caledonia. Solid ground wove under his feet as if he were still on the ship. His stomach lurched several times off-loading gear and supplies. Twenty-four hours later, he continued to feel a bit queasy. Sweat dripped constantly from his head in the high humidity, adding to the discomfort of the jungle-covered island.

He carried a galvanized steel mess tray with the grayish mystery meat from his C ration can. He missed his mom's china, her food, and even the dumpy place where they lived. His new home, a large house-like tent with a hastily laid wooden board floor, depressed him. He didn't know what he had expected from the Army, but this certainly wasn't it.

The field team worked on building a mess unit as fast as they could. Considering sporadic supply drops, he didn't hold out hope for hot, normal food anytime soon. They had potatoes, carrots, and onions but not much else—other than what the men hunted in the jungle. Wild pig and snake seemed the order of the day. Bernard gagged the first time a Southern boy said snake tasted like chicken.

"Howard, your platoon is scheduled for hunt duty tonight." The sergeant flipped through a clipboard full of pages curled from humidity.

There's a new guy named Howard?

"Howard!" The sergeant kicked Bernard on the side of his boot.

Bernard jumped. He dumped the tray on the floor. The meat held together in a gelatinous lump.

"This slop is better spread on the floor than in your gut," said the sergeant. "You've got hunt duty, Howard."

Seven weeks in the army and he still wasn't used to being called by his surname.

"Yes, sir . . . er, Sergeant?" Bernard asked. "What is hunt duty?"

The seasoned veterans of the island snorted with laughter.

"On better thought, you new guys ought to be indoctrinated into other squads. If I sent you out in the jungle alone, you might never find your way back." The sergeant scribbled on the page and crossed out a few lines.

Bernard had learned nothing about hunting back at Fort Dix, but most of what he had learned hadn't been useful thus far. Considering the broken-down, ancient equipment, mechanical repair classes would have been more helpful.

"Jenson, Dunkle, and Souter, you go with the first squad tonight. Howard, Griffith, and Higgins, you go with third squad tomorrow night," said the sergeant.

Jenson had just entered the tent house with a canvas water bucket.

The sergeant looked up from his clipboard. "Okay, guys, fill up, especially you guys going out with us tonight."

Jenson set the bucket on the floor, flipped the molded metal cup from the top of his quart canteen, and submerged the canteen in the bucket until it filled. Dunkle and Souter followed suit.

Bernard chugged most of his almost-full canteen and filled it again. "What's hunt duty about? We didn't learn that in basic."

The sun sank below the horizon, and the jungle slipped into twilight. Bugs and critters didn't mind the human interruption. They sang their evening songs.

Dunkle sharpened a long polished machete with a sharpening stone working the leading edge of the blade. "That's our meat source until Uncle sends provisions."

"Unless you want to live on those cans of C rations," said Souter, pointing to the stack of cases in the corner of the tent. "The only thing worth having is the toilet paper and cigarettes."

"They have mystery meat, pork, ham, or chicken. Fresh meat rules the roost," said Dunkle with a smile as he continued slicing the stone along the blade. "We catch wild pigs and snakes."

A movement in the corner of the tent caught Bernard's eye. He moved closer, then backed away fast, grabbed his haversack, and drew back to pitch it at the offender.

"Whoa," said Souter, extending a hand to stop Bernard. He walked to the corner, bent down, and rose with a small reptile wrapped around his fingers. "It's just a gargoyle gecko. They're harmless." He stroked the small creature's back as he walked to the doorway and deposited it outside the tent.

Bernard cringed. An involuntary shiver ran along his back. He tried not to let on how much it bothered him. "I don't like lizards and I hate snakes."

The rest of the men chuckled.

"Don't laugh. When I was six, we lived in the country and I fell into a sinkhole where a couple dozen snakes were trapped. By the time my parents found me, I had half a dozen bites on my body." Sweat popped through on his forehead. His heart pounded at the recollection. "There was no way to get away from them slithering and striking at me. I wasn't able to talk for days." Bernard looked around at the unsympathetic, smiling faces and felt a sudden vulnerability.

The night was heavy with moisture, and the men were exhausted from a hard day's work clearing jungle for a landing strip. Bernard drifted off to sleep as soon as they got the okay to bunk down. He hadn't even stripped down to his skivvies. He lay across his bunk in full uniform, his snores drowning out most of the nocturnal sounds around him.

Close to midnight, Griffith and Higgins sat at the scruffy wooden table in the corner, playing poker by lantern light. They looked up at the same time. Shuffling sounds came closer to the tent. The door burst open. Jenson, Dunkle, and Souter poured into the room, wrestling with a sea snake spread out among the three of them.

Souter laughed out loud. "This is the biggest one we've caught so far. It should make for real good eats."

"Tastes like chicken," said Dunkle, the country boy from Georgia. His nappy head looked almost comical with all the jungle twigs and refuse captured in his hair.

"Shhh," cautioned Jenson. "You'll wake Howard."

He had the lead, holding onto the snake's head. He maneuvered the other two in the direction of Bernard's bunk.

"Man, leave Howard alone," mumbled Higgins. He sucked a long draw on the unfiltered cigarette clenched between his lips as he sorted his cards.

Souter tried to pull back on the end he was holding but Jenson wouldn't stop. He approached the bunk. Bernard's face was to the tent wall and his back to the men. Jenson hurled the snake onto the sleeping man, yanking it from the other men's hands.

The snake slithered across Bernard's shoulders, and its head disappeared around his neck. The men exploded in laughter. In his sleep, Bernard swatted at the movement around his head. His legs kicked and he bolted upright on the bed. It only took him a second to realize he was entangled in a mass of moving skin. He lunged off his cot, flailing and screaming.

Jenson fell to his bunk in laughter. Griffith and Higgins just shook their heads and went back to playing cards.

"Snake!" Bernard fell off the bed, pulling the snake off with him. He kicked at it, which seemed to tighten the length of undulating flesh around his legs.

His heart pounded like a bass drum and drowned out his screams. An attack by a monster. Could it wrap around him and squeeze him to death? He kicked at it. Pushing with both hands, but afraid to touch the disgusting thing. The scales undulated under his hands. His breath came in short bursts as he tried to get away, but his feet couldn't get traction.

The snake decided it wanted to be somewhere else and tried to slither away. Souter caught it by the head and with one sweeping chop of his machete beheaded the creature. Now both parts were writhing and wiggling. Bernard jumped to his feet. Anger flooded his chest.

"Who did that?" Rage shot from his eyes, and a small amount of spittle collected in the right corner of his mouth.

Dunkle corralled the moving snake parts and headed for the door as he pointed at Jenson, who was spread out on his bed laughing.

Bernard lunged for him and landed square on his chest. He punched Jenson in the face. They locked in combat and rolled to the floor in a flurry of arms and legs.

Griffith and Higgins scrambled from their seats to stop the fight, each holding one of the men.

Jenson tried to pull loose from Higgins. "What's your problem, Howard! It was a joke. You're bad news, man."

Bernard's eyes drilled into Jenson's face. "I told you before, I hate snakes." He jerked his arms free of Griffith and paced. "Why do you have to be such a fathead?"

Griffith held out both hands and stood between the men. "Don't you two think we have enough problems in this place without being jerks to each other? They already think we're not capable of anything other than menial labor. Do you want them to think we have no civility?"

Higgins released his grip on Jenson and returned to the table. He seated himself and leaned his elbows on his knees. "They decided Negro soldiers were going to face the enemy at the wheel of a truck or behind a shovel long before we got here. Don't try to pretend our stupid fight is the reason we don't have any Negro officers in the whole battalion."

"Let's face it," said Jenson, who straightened his uniform, stepped back a ways, but remained defiant. "This is just as dangerous, if not more, than combat. We basically built the airfield with no help from the higher-ups, using only broken-down World War I heavy equipment we have to hold together with spit and Band-Aids." He jammed a fist into the back of a chair and sent it flying. "And this place was the center of the fighting last year for the Solomons campaign. We lost dozens of guys because of faulty equipment or the jungle. But we did it, built the roads and infrastructure the Navy needed to keep their carrier *Enterprise* in the fight. Did we get any credit? No."

The tension of the moment was diverted to the real problem trying to claw its way to the surface for all the men—the lack of respect for them as soldiers.

Bernard had been reluctant to voice an opinion since he was one of the new guys. "Is it true the white soldiers in the section of the battalion stationed at the Noumea Port and north of there are getting more pay than we are?"

Jenson sagged to his bunk. "The EABs aren't even getting as much as the white soldiers."

"What are EABs?" asked Bernard. His head was full of such a large number of terms he kept forgetting the ones he didn't use regularly.

Souter, who'd retreated to his bunk at the beginning of the skirmish, spoke. "Engineering Aviation Battalions. They do runway construction and repair. Those guys get all the great equipment and we get bupkus."

"They deserve it," said Dunkle. He strolled back into the tent.

Bernard backed away from him in case he had a snake hidden behind his back.

Dunkle held out empty hands.

Bernard relaxed.

"The first two units out of the states were the 810th and 811th. Last year when they arrived, their equipment was backlogged for three weeks, therefore they unloaded cargo ships at Noumea. Most of the time they were under Japanese bombing attacks. Then they had to trek over a hundred miles to Plaines des Galacs. They cleared trees, built roads, and bridges on the way," said Dunkle.

"Yeah, but they had the airfield ready in time for the Battle of the Coral Sea," said Souter. A smile of satisfaction spread across his face. "It was a job well done, especially when none of the brass thought they could do it."

It was the second time Bernard had seen Souter smile since he'd arrived in New Caledonia. The first time was when he let Souter borrow his Bible. Bernard ran his hand across his head, the snake forgotten. "You guys have been in this backward situation for a long time, and I've seen numerous Negro war correspondents, so I know they must be writing about it. Why didn't we know this back home?"

Griffith shook his head and snorted a chuckle like a sneeze. "The wartime censors would pull their credentials if they started spreading the word about how it really is here. Believe me, Jim Crow is alive and well in the United States Army."

A banging sound like a spoon hitting a pot invaded the tent. The men quit the conversation in mid-sentence and headed for the door. Bernard followed behind.

19

March 10, 1943

Cordelia sat on the couch in the living room, numb to the events of the day. She stared down at her gloved hands. She was uncomfortable in the warmth of the house, yet she couldn't bring herself to move. Could her willpower suspend time, make things go back to the way they were? Why had this happened? Were her own words at fault? Questions swirled in her conscious thoughts, paralyzing her emotions.

She wished she could take back the hurtful words. She wished she had said good-bye. Grammy's words popped into her head. *If wishes were fishes, the oceans would be full.*

She hadn't cried yet, but tears threatened to destroy her stoic façade. It was over and done. The mortuary would have held the bodies over until spring, but Cordelia opted for cremation. At least she didn't have to go to a graveside service.

"Okay, that's the last of them. Everyone's gone home." Gertie hurried back into the room. "Now you can get some rest. How are you feeling?"

The wall fell. Cordelia lifted her chin, and a river of tears streamed down her cheeks, splashed onto the front of her black wool dress, and soaked in as fast as they landed. It struck her that the tears were like her parents. So important for a moment in time, but gone in an instant.

"Oh, honey," Gertie scooted onto the couch beside her and wrapped her arms around the crying girl's shoulders. "I'm so sorry."

"What am I going to do? This is my fault," wailed Cordelia.

Gertie held her at arm's length. "Why is it your fault?"

Cordelia mumbled.

Gertie tipped her head up. "What?"

"Because I wished them dead," said Cordelia. Sobs wracked her shoulders as she dropped her head back into her gloved hands. "And now this nightmare has happened."

"Oh, baby, it's not your fault." Gertie smoothed away the wet hair plastered to Cordelia's forehead.

Cordelia ripped off her gloves and threw them across the floor. There was no one left to tell her she had to pick them up. Gertie jumped at her outburst.

"What am I going to do now? There's no one left in our—my family. I'm rolling around in this house all by myself." She could hide in her bedroom and avoid the world while she recovered from the shock.

"Don't you have a grandfather, your mom's father, left?"

"Yes, but I haven't seen him in years. Mom didn't talk to him. They had some kind of falling out. I don't even know where he lives."

A knock. Cordelia froze, remembering the last time. The knock that had exploded her world.

Gertie held out both hands. "I'll get it. You stay put."

Cordelia offered a feeble protest. She didn't have the strength to argue. She sank back onto the couch as the front door ruckus gravitated to the living room.

"I'm sure you could wait. She just said good-bye to her parents an hour ago," said Gertie. Cordelia knew the tone. Gertie's voice dropped an octave when she held her anger in check.

Mr. Bennett, the head of the church operating Board, brushed past Gertie. He took off his hat as he entered the living room. "Miss Grace, the church advisory Board wishes to express our sincere condolences at the loss of your parents." He looked down at his hat.

Gertie stepped around him. "Thank you, Mr. Bennett, but this was expressed quite sufficiently at the service. I beg to ask—"

"Why are you here?" asked Cordelia with a tone as dead as her parents. Her eyes burned with fatigue. Her father was no longer here to rein her in, and she didn't have to play games with church people anymore.

Gertie returned to the couch.

Bennett shuffled his feet as though he were searching for the appropriate words. "I'm sure you can appreciate the church's willingness to allow you to remain in this house."

Cordelia stiffened. "But . . ."

Bennett bit the side of his lip. "But we need you to vacate the premises by the end of the month."

Gertie jumped to her feet. "That's really a low blow. Her parents just died."

"We have a new pastor and his family coming from Illinois, and this is the parsonage."

Cordelia had lived here her whole life. She forgot it didn't belong to her parents. Her mind swirled. What would she do? Where would she go?

"I'll need time," said Cordelia. "I have to find someone to move all of the furniture."

Bennett pulled an envelope-sized folder from inside his suit jacket breast pocket. "Which brings me to the next order of business." He held out the folder. "Your father was borrowing money from the church Board. He mortgaged all the furniture and its contents to the church for the debt."

"Wait a minute," said Gertie. "Didn't the church pay for an insurance policy or something for the pastor?"

Bennett looked embarrassed. "The church Board could only afford one or the other . . . the insurance or the loan. He chose the loan." He continued to hold out the folder.

The folder hung from the end of his hand, suspended in time. If she didn't touch it, did it really exist?

Cordelia felt the blood drain from her face as she reached for the folder. The room shifted in her vision and her hands turned to ice as she unfolded the document and scanned the page. "So you're telling me I'm penniless and don't own anything left in the house?"

Bennett hung his head again. "That would be correct. I . . . we, can only allow you to take your personal possessions when you leave."

Gertie came nose-to-nose with Bennett. "I take it you wonderfully compassionate people are kicking her out on her ear?"

"I'm sure you can appreciate—"

Her strength returned. "I don't appreciate anything at this point in my life, but you can bet I'll be out of *your* house by the end of today." Cordelia turned to leave but stopped short and turned back. "And forgive me if I don't take the time to dust the house or do the dishes." And with that, she turned on her heels and stormed from the room.

Mr. Bennett must have informed his wife that Cordelia was leaving immediately because she and a crew of the ladies from the church arrived two hours later to start cleaning. Cordelia and Gertie packed her clothes in her mother's good luggage. At least she wouldn't have to leave the luggage.

Mrs. Bennett approached the door of Cordelia's bedroom as she gathered her luggage. She made a beeline for the bed and Cordelia's quilt. She picked it up. "Oh, what a lovely Pinecone Quilt—"

Cordelia snatched it from her hands. "It belongs to me, and it's not staying." As she handed it off to Gertie, a slight smirk graced her friend's lips.

Mrs. Bennett looked a little taken aback. "Sorry, dearie, but—"

"Excuse me if I don't have time for chitchat. I have to find a place to live." Cordelia grabbed her bags and Grammy's Bible from the stripped bed. She bolted for the front door. She waited for Gertie to struggle through with her full load and then intentionally slammed the door behind her.

"I think you made this move a little too fast," said Gertie.

"I couldn't help myself. I don't know what's gotten into me lately. I think I needed to feel like I had some control of the situation, but my control consists of me being homeless at the moment."

"You're welcome to stay with me until you figure this out."

Cordelia turned and smiled. "Thanks for sticking by me. I'm a mess, aren't I?"

Gertie looked at her sideways. "I'm glad you said it so I didn't have to. What do you want to tackle first?"

"Well, I guess I need a job." She looked sad again. "I'm going to have to quit school. I have no way to support myself very long without a full-time job."

"I can help with that, too," said Gertie. "They're hiring at the factory. Today's Wednesday and I bet you could start tomorrow."

"I'll need to have Bernard's mom let me get his letters at her house until I figure out where I'm going to live."

Gertie stopped at the bottom of the walk. The snow had stopped but the air was still frosty. "Not that I don't want you to stay with me, because I surely do, but what kind of relationship do you have with Bernard's parents?"

Cordelia puckered her lips. "Hardly any, why?"

"Well, you are practically their daughter-in-law, and they do have Bernard's room empty—"

"Oh, no, I couldn't."

"Why couldn't you?"

"Because . . ." Cordelia didn't want to openly express fear of Bernard's father because he had never done anything to her personally.

"That's what I thought. Let's go." Gertie traipsed down the street toward the Court, with Cordelia scrambling to follow in the slippery snow.

It had all happened too fast. She should go home with Gertie for a while. Cordelia faced the front of the gate of Bernard's house.

Gertie opened the gate, climbed the stairs, and set Cordelia's suitcases on the porch. "Do you want me to wait and see if they're okay with you staying?"

"No, I'll be okay," Cordelia said swiftly. She figured when Gertie left, then she could scram out of there. But where would she go if she didn't go with Gertie?

"Okay. See you in the morning at the factory. I'll tell them you are coming," said Gertie as she bounded down the stairs and out into the Court.

"Wait." Cordelia turned. Or was this the right thing to do?

"Cordelia, is that you, dear?" Anna Howard opened the door. She looked down the stairs at Cordelia holding a suitcase, and then at the two suitcases sitting on her porch.

"Yes, ma'am, it's me." How do you ask your fiancée's mother for a place to stay?

"Well, come in, dear, before you catch your death . . ." Anna flushed at her choice of words. She lifted the two suitcases and hauled them into the house.

Bernard's father. Her chest tightened. This wasn't such a good idea.

"The neighborhood grapevine says your father's church Board threw you out of their house." Anna set the suitcases inside the living room door.

Cordelia hung her head. The neighborhood knew before she did. "Yes, ma'am."

How should she ask for lodging? Her heart skipped a beat at living near Bernard's father because of his meanness, but she feared homelessness more.

Anna wrapped her arms around Cordelia's shoulders and drew her toward the living room. "It's all right, my dear girl. You're welcome in our home. Bernard would never forgive us if we left you out in the world alone."

Cordelia stopped short. Charles Howard sat on the far end of the couch reading a newspaper. She tried to back out of the room.

Anna stopped her with a firm hand. "My husband and I have discussed this, haven't we, Charles?"

"You're welcome to stay in Bernard's room," said Charles with his eyes trained on the newspaper page. "But we can't afford any more mouths to feed. You're going to have to support yourself."

Cordelia trembled. She couldn't distinguish relief from fear, but at the moment she was grateful. She set her bags down, but clutched the quilt to her chest. "Thank you, Mr. Howard. I'm getting a job at Day Hollow Manufacturing tomorrow."

Charles set his jaw and folded the paper. "Well, it's a good start. You can call me Charles. Mr. Howard was my father."

"Yes, sir . . . Mr. Charles." Her knees shook. She'd be in the same house, for most of her days, with the man she had grown to fear.

"Come sit down, child," said Anna as she brushed Cordelia's hair away from her shoulders. "I'm sorry for your loss."

A scream welled up inside her to correct Anna's choice of words. She tamped it back down. This time she had lost—everything.

Charles rose from the couch and climbed the stairs without speaking.

Anna led Cordelia to the vacated couch. Cordelia laid the quilt on the cushion. She pulled off her coat and draped it on the other side of her.

"Your quilt is beautiful." Anna ran her hand across the pattern. "How long have you been working on it?"

Cordelia's face warmed. Was she catching a cold or was she embarrassed? "I've been working on it since last year, when my Grammy died. She started it for me."

"Did you see the one I made?" Anna pointed at the one gracing the back of the couch.

"Yes, I saw it one of the times I was here. You do very nice needlework."

Anna smiled. "It's more than needlework, my dear."

"I know; it's a mantle of prayers for my life." Cordelia mimicked her grandmother's voice.

Anna raised an eyebrow. "I think those words sound a tad sarcastic."

"I'm sorry." Cordelia chewed on her lip, but the words flooded out. "My Grammy kept saying those prayers were going to cover my life. I haven't had a single good thing happen since she started this quilt. I've lost everything I hold dear. I wasn't sold on the prayer bit to start with—"

"You've gotten the wrong impression of a Pinecone Quilt."

20

April 10, 1943

Cordelia sat cross-legged on Bernard's bed with her quilt spread across her legs. She'd stitched enough rows on the circular pattern to make it almost as wide as the bed. As it grew, each row took longer to complete, but a renewed purpose blossomed.

Anna had been a godsend. They bonded immediately and gave Cordelia a new sense of peace. Anna explained prayer as Holy Spirit intervention.

Cordelia understood her part in the full circle. Bernard had helped his mom. Now his mom helped Cordelia. She was going to pray him home if it was the last thing she ever did.

Anna tapped on the door. "Cordelia, are you still awake, honey?"

Cordelia's bedside table clock read almost eleven. "Yes, ma'am." She yawned.

Anna opened the door. "I'm sorry. I was lying down when you got home from work. I had a headache. Did you find the dinner I left in the oven?" She sat on the edge of the bed.

"Yes, I found it. You are too good to me. Thank you."

"You are going to be my daughter-in-law, and I love you like my child."

Cordelia stitched. "Did you see the batch of letters I got from Bernard?"

Anna smiled. "Yes, that's why I came, to see what he had to say." Since she had moved in, he always wrote one side of the paper to Cordelia and the other to his mom to save on postage.

Anna reached in the sewing basket on the nightstand for the needle she used to work on the quilt. She focused on the unfinished end of the row opposite Cordelia.

Cordelia motioned to the dresser. "They're over there. Help yourself. He addressed it to both of us this time, instead of separate sides. He's glad I'm staying with you, but he told me to avoid his father."

Anna moved her needle expertly to secure the fabric. "Charles would never hurt you. There's things Bernard never knew. Sometimes we have to learn to look through the meanness to their pain."

Cordelia froze. A shiver ran along her spine. It was a while ago, but she remembered. Those were Grammy's exact words when they talked about the Wilson kids.

"Is something wrong, child?"

Cordelia shook her head while her insides shook, too. "No, ma'am. Grammy used to say the same thing about other people's pain."

"It's a hard lesson to learn, but we all need to walk a mile in someone else's shoes before we condemn them about anything."

Cordelia turned pensive.

"But enough about other folks. How is my son doing? You tell me. My head is still powerful pained from the headache, and my eyes are a little blurry."

"Well, sure enough he's wishing for a bunch of your peaches."

They both laughed.

"He told us about some nasty food called C rations, which have ham, eggs, and potatoes already cooked in a can. The pork and beans didn't sound too bad, but it sounds downright nasty to eat the stuff cold," said Cordelia as she folded a square of material.

Anna looked shocked. "Land's sakes. They have to eat cold food?"

"He said they have those little Sterno cans to heat the stuff with, but still. I guess they're out in the field building stuff quite often and they can't get a lot of hot meals. He did say something about a pig roast, but I don't have any idea where they'd get a pig from if they only have canned food."

"I've been afraid to ask, but is my boy safe?"

"I asked, and he said the fighting has moved away from them. They're the main supply system for the Asian Pacific campaign. It doesn't look like there will be any more battles there."

"Praise Jesus." Anna held a square in her hand. Her lips moved with silent words, and then she sewed the piece into place.

Cordelia watched. "I hope you realize you've given me a new sense of purpose."

Anna blushed. "Me? Why do you say that?"

"Because I was being stubborn. Or it could be I was too immature when Grammy started with me, but you really helped me understand this." She gestured to the quilt.

"Well, my ma always taught us to look at the quilt like a living diary. Instead of keeping all those hopes and dreams locked in a book, you spread them out here in the pattern to help you see them every day. Each one answered is another reason to build your faith."

"I think my problem was I didn't hear all Grammy's prayers. I don't know if they were answered or not."

"Have you prayed any of your own, child?"

"Yes, ma'am." Cordelia blushed. "Most of mine are about Bernard. Some of the things I prayed against happened anyhow."

"Not every prayer is going to get the answer you want, in the way you want. Remember, the Lord has a much bigger plan than our little minds could ever understand."

Cordelia marveled at Anna's understanding of Scripture. "Did you learn all of this from Bernard?"

Anna laughed out loud. "No. I'm actually the person Bernard learned it from, but I fell away from the Lord. I was lost in my own pain, and it took my son to bring me out of it. My husband is the same way, but he hasn't recovered yet."

"Yet? You say 'yet'?"

She nodded. "Yes, because I believe in the Lord for his healing, too."

Anna helped Cordelia for about an hour, then left to go back to bed. Cordelia wasn't tired, and she didn't plan on going to church the next morning. The sour taste in her mouth had her looking for another church to join. She hoped she might be able to get Anna to go to a new church with her.

Her tongue stuck to the roof of her mouth and her stomach emitted a tiny grumble. Iced tea and Anna's oatmeal cookies sounded good. There were still a few left in the bread bin. She hopped off the bed and slid into her robe and slippers.

She turned on the lamp at the bottom of the stairs. She stopped short. Charles, without a T-shirt, stood by the open door of the refrigerator, drinking cold water from his favorite glass bottle.

She gasped involuntarily and tried to divert her eyes but couldn't turn from the sight. The man's back looked like beaten meat. Elongated healed-over gouges jumbled in darkened scars across his flesh. Where pigment hadn't returned, pink and mottled slash marks hatched across some of the older wounds. Her stomach heaved.

Charles lowered the water bottle and turned his head toward her. "I heard you, but I thought you were Anna." He slid the bottle back onto the wire shelf, closed the door, and turned to face her. He looked visibly embarrassed. "I'm sorry. I didn't realize you were still awake or I wouldn't have come down without a shirt."

His head lowered as he started for the kitchen door.

Cordelia held her ground, bolstered by the evidence of savagery she'd just seen. "What happened to your back?" Was he in some kind of a horrible accident Bernard hadn't mentioned? The thought passed. Bernard always told her everything.

Charles stopped. "Why?" He acted defensive and uncomfortable.

"Because your back looks like it's been chewed in a meat grinder." Cordelia planted both feet . . . as though she could stop him.

"I was raised in Alabama. Jim Crow laws are alive and well down there. When you tend to disregard them, there are consequences." Charles couldn't get by Cordelia. He pulled out a chair and sat.

Cordelia winced. "People beat you? For what reason?" She seated herself across the table from him. Her hands shook, but she rested them on the table.

"Defiance of what they considered the orderly way of life. Back in the day, we couldn't even use the front door to the grocery store. We were supposed to go around in the alley and ask for what we wanted to buy."

"But it was in the olden days, and down South. It's not that way here in Scranton today."

Charles clasped his hands together and shut his lips tight.

"What are you saying? Or not saying?" Cordelia tried to look in his eyes but he had lowered his head. "Look at me, please." She didn't know she could be forceful.

Charles lifted his head and stared into her eyes. She resisted shrinking back. *In for a penny, in for a pound.* She gulped. "Some of your scars look recent. Did they happen here?"

"Let's just say two guys weren't happy with a Negro getting a job in the coal mines. They thought it was going to one of their friends."

Her eyes widened as her hand flew to her mouth to stifle a cry. "Did you go to the police? Those men need to be arrested. Were there any witnesses?"

"These aren't the kind of things you go to the police about."

"Well, I've always been taught the police are the line between the laws and the lawbreakers."

"Well, it works if you're alive for the outcome."

"They threatened your life?"

"Only if I wouldn't quit."

"But you didn't quit. You still work—"

Charles shook his head.

The details clicked into place. "Now I understand why I saw you taking out the garbage at the Ritz Theatre." Thank goodness she hadn't told Bernard. The hand of the Lord was in what had happened to her.

"Listen, girl." Charles placed both palms on the table. "I don't know why I'm telling you my business. Bernard is not to know about this conversation, especially while he's away from home. Only Anna knows what I'm tellin' ya."

Cordelia nodded. "I promise." She saw a whole different person from the man she thought she knew. She needed to start praying for this man. His burdens were far beyond what she ever imagined. She understood now what Anna meant about praying continually for Charles. All this time Cordelia thought the prayers were to keep him from beating her, but instead, the prayers were to heal his heart and mind.

"I felt real bad about it, but it's the reason why Bernard had to quit school. I couldn't find enough odd jobs to keep our heads above water. I've got a pretty good circuit of work now, but I'm not sure how long it will last after the war is over."

She could hear Grammy again . . . *Sometimes we have to learn to look through the meanness to their pain.* Cordelia rubbed her hand across her mouth. The words wouldn't form. She wasn't sure of what to say. "Sorry" seemed a bit superficial.

21

November 9, 1943

Bernard sat at the rough-cut table in the corner of his tent home. Out in the jungle they were cutting trails, building roads, or landing spots, but at the end of the day, coming *home* kept them going. He looked around for the occasional living creature that invaded the space. None evident at the moment.

He pulled the envelope from his shirt pocket. He'd read Cordelia's letter three times, but he wanted to read it once more before he wrote to her. His letters were getting shorter and shorter, but there wasn't anything pleasant about this place he wanted to share. The last time he wrote he wanted to share about the pig roast. But how do you tell your city girl-friend how a bunch of guys hacked a wild pig to death with machetes? Better left unsaid, like most things around here.

He'd lost a good ten pounds since his arrival. He lived on mostly the C rations. The other men ate from the hunt, but Bernard couldn't bring himself to eat snake in any form.

Souter came into the tent with a mess plate of stew. He set the plate on the table and rummaged through the pile of C ration boxes until he found a can of biscuits. "Don't you want any stew?"

Bernard looked at it. He could see potatoes and carrots in nice-sized chunks. The onion aroma floated in his direction. It didn't smell half bad. Without asking more, Bernard rose and went outside.

The platoon formed a line with mess kits in hands. At the head of the group stood the mess sergeant with his makeshift stove, a fire surrounded by a couple of cinderblocks. On top of the blocks sat a galvanized steel, twenty-gallon garbage can—apparently full of stew. Bernard went back into the tent.

"I'd rather eat C rations than eat out of a garbage can," said Bernard as he rummaged through the pile of cans looking for pork and beans.

"The garbage can is a cook pot big enough for the whole platoon," said Souter as he shoveled the food in his mouth by the forkful.

"I'm not eating out of a garbage can." Why did the white soldiers stationed in Noumea have real buildings and a real mess hall while the Negroes anguished in transient buildings with promises of permanent structures. Some of the guys in the platoon had been here since the Solomons campaign last year and still lived under the same promises.

"It's never been used for garbage. Man, you wouldn't survive down home. We use them for picnic spreads all the time."

Bernard made a face as though he smelled something bad. "I'm not eating it. But I should have asked what the meat is. I know there were no meat rations in the last supply drop."

Souter chuckled. "Nope, no meat, but they sure got enough cases of beer."

Bernard knitted his brow.

"I know you're not one to be tipping the elbow, but you gotta remember this is one of the only pleasures we get. Well, that and the women in town. I don't think it's the least bit fair the white soldiers get to go to Australia for R and R, and we get bupkus."

"All they have there is kangaroos and sand. We got sand here. Don't worry about it." Bernard wanted to keep the men's heads on the job and not focused on the discrimination. It was getting tough for him. "They need to let those women alone, especially Jenson. He's going to get in trouble with all those ladies."

Souter burst out laughing. "Jenson has had at least six girlfriends since he got here more than a year ago. The dark-haired one named Sonia keeps saying she's going back to the States with him."

"Sure. I could see his wife and his mother loving that. The boy needs to repent and find the Lord." Bernard hadn't cracked his Bible open in a couple of months. He needed to repent, too.

"I'll let him know tonight at the beer party, since I know you won't be there," said Souter.

"If I did drink, which I don't, warm beer doesn't sound like much of a party."

"The beer will be good and cold. They hit the cases with CO_2 fire extinguishers. It cools them off right fast."

Bernard never did find out what type of meat was in the stew. He decided he didn't really want to know.

The makeshift alarm sounded with a banging pot and spoon. This time Bernard scrambled from the table at the same time Souter shoveled in his last forkful of food. They both headed for the door.

22

June 6, 1944

D-Day

Cordelia trudged down the alley to Day Hollow Manufacturing. She was tired from the long day of work, but in all the excitement she'd forgotten her bag with the quilt in it. She had brought it in to show Gertie her progress. Since Gertie had switched to second shift at the beginning of the year to earn more money, they didn't get a lot of time to see each other anymore.

Not that she was complaining. She loved Gertie, but she cherished the relationship she and Anna had built over the last year and a half. She had learned how to cook, can fruits and vegetables, and the real hands-on process of sewing clothes. Anna's treadle sewing machine provided fascinating weekends making curtains and clothes whenever they could get extra material.

But the excitement today eclipsed everything. Today the Allies had invaded Normandy. Even as she walked in Scranton, soldiers fought for a fifty-mile stretch of French beaches called Utah, Omaha, Gold, Juno, and Sword. This could be a turning point in the war. Bernard would come home.

She worried about him. Though he appeared to be safe, he was changing. Nothing specific she could put her finger on, but his letters had changed. Last year there were two, some-times three, sheets of paper. Now his letters barely filled one sheet and conveyed no playfulness or humor.

She slid the delivery door open on its track. The heat whooshed into her face. After dark, the interior would cool off some, but it was sweltering during the day with the sun beating on the tin roof. She maneuvered between narrow, bin-clogged aisles to her row of machines near the wall. Gertie was in the night section at the other end of the plant. She could hear their machines running but couldn't see them.

Vinnie, the shop steward, held her quilt. Her heart thumped. What was he doing in her things? She bolted for her machine.

"It belongs to me, Vinnie. I came back to get it." She reached for the quilt.

He dangled it out of her reach.

"This is pretty nice. My mother would like something this nice."

"Well, she'll just have to get someone to make her one." Cordelia reached for it again.

Vinnie grabbed her wrist. "I don't think this quilt is as important as your job. What do you think?"

Cordelia backed away a step. He didn't let go. She winced. "What do you mean?"

Vinnie's sinister grin caused Cordelia's heartbeat to tick up another notch.

"If you want this, there's something I should get for it. It's in my family's factory."

"Like what?" She wrenched her hand free of his fat fingers and backed further away.

He draped the quilt across the bin as though he were mak-ing a bed. "I don't know, maybe you should spend some time with me in my office." He smoothed out the quilt.

Cordelia shook her head. "No, I won't do it. And you can't make me. I'll tell your father." She eyed the quilt. Did she have enough room to snatch it and run? It'd grown heavy and to almost a full size. She wouldn't be able to run and carry it. She would fight for it if necessary, but it might cost her her job.

Vinnie threw his head back and laughed. "And you think my father would believe you, the little Negro girl?" He reached to touch her again.

A push broom handle slapped down on his raised arm, pinning it to the quilt. Vinnie yowled in pain.

"He might not believe her, but he'd believe me," said Charles Howard. He was wieldeing his push broom as a weapon. Two years of night maintenance, hauling bins and loading trucks, built great arm strength. His biceps strained at the thin material of his worn T-shirt.

Vinnie jerked his arm from under the broom, then clutched it to his chest. "You crazy n—"

"I wouldn't say that if you value where your nose is sitting," said Charles.

Vinnie stammered with the words, looking at the broom handle poised to swipe at him.

Charles turned to Cordelia. "Take your quilt and go home, girl."

Cordelia gathered the quilt, shoved it in her bag, and darted out of the factory. Her legs quivered like those of a newborn calf trying to stand but she walked faster. Her heart beat against her rib cage, but she could almost smile.

23

Bernard slashed his way through the dense jungle foliage with the sharpened machete. The midmorning sun beat down with enough ferocity to cause dew on the jungle floor to turn into steam. The men who developed allergies in this climate couldn't breathe easily in the thick moist air. It didn't bother Bernard.

Several of the guys in his squad said his grim tone while cutting undergrowth was enough to scare away even the humidity and that was the reason he didn't get allergies. He personally didn't see the humor in their opinion, but there wasn't much he found humorous these days. A year and a half of deliberate segregation, constant humiliation at the hands of noncommissioned officers, particularly the sergeants they had to deal with, who thought his race inferior, and less than adequate supplies and accommodations all worked together to make him bitter.

He slashed at the broad leaves with a vengeance. Less than adequate wasn't the correct terminology to describe their barracks. Separate but equal for the Negro troops? Someone forgot to tell the construction crews who left the materials. Yes, the Negro boys were used to building something from nothing, and they still accomplished the job. But there were still night-and-day differences between the quality of the accommodations.

The announcement filtered down this morning that troops at Normandy were expecting a rousing success. Hopefully he could get out of this forsaken place and go home. He stopped and wiped the sweat from his forehead with the bandana from his back pocket. He pulled a cigarette from the pack in his rolled sleeve and with a flick of his thumbnail struck a match. Several long drags calmed him. He looked at the filterless tobacco stick hanging between his fingers. He'd have to abandon this nasty habit before he went home. His mom and Cordelia would have a bird if they knew he smoked.

The banging pot sounded through the thicket to the barracks. Sometimes he wished he could take a sledgehammer to that thing. It was never good news.

"What now?" muttered Bernard. He grabbed the machete and laid the flat blade across his shoulder as he navigated the bush. Who's in trouble now?

He crested the hill and hoofed it into the clearing as the rest of the platoon assembled outside the rickety mess hall.

"Who got drunk in town last night?" Bernard asked a buddy.

Drinking was the closest thing they had to R and R, other than an occasional new baseball so they could start another team. The men snuck off every now and then to make hay while the sun shined, or in more precise terms . . . while the moon shined. The drill went . . . they snuck out, wound up snockered, fought, then received *rehabilitation* for several days in the military pokey.

He counted heads. The only one missing seemed to be Jenson. Bernard shook his head. Jenson, at it again. How did he keep all of those girls interested? Well, on second thought he did understand, but it wasn't something he wanted to dwell on.

Bernard smelled his own sweat, and the dirt clung to him from working on the new latrine. He wanted a decent shower but would settle for the dribble their broken-down pump produced. Jenson had been in this predicament before and it wouldn't be the last time. Bernard started to walk back to the barracks.

The noncom hopped into the back of the M35 cargo truck. Bernard's squad had used the two-and-a-half-ton truck to haul tall supplies the day before, so the tarp had been removed. The headroom allowed the sergeant to stand in the deuce and a half without squatting.

"We've handed out pamphlets to you boys about not fraternizing with the local women or any military females on the island," said the straight-faced sergeant.

"Well, who does it leave for us to make nice with, Sarge?" One of the men from squad three grinned as though he'd made a great joke.

The noncom lowered the clipboard. "No one. The ramifications of deliberate fraternization can be severe."

"What'd he say?" asked Souter.

"He means you're going to get your butt in a sling if you make nice with any of the honeys on this island," said Bernard.

"When will Jenson be back?" asked Bernard. He'd have to fill in on Jenson's latrine duty if they were going to get this new section done. Jenson would likely pay his two days and be back in a flash.

"He won't be back," said the noncom.

Bernard stopped and turned back. "Why not?"

The noncom turned the page on the board and ran his finger down the column. "He's being held over for court-martial."

The men crowded forward.

Bernard pushed his way back through the group. "Court-martial? For what? How did he get in that much trouble in less than eight hours?"

"He's being charged with rape."

The men all started talking at once. Bernard raised a hand to quiet them. "Who's he supposed to have raped?" Bernard wanted to name off all his girlfriends, but it might make the situation worse.

"The girl runs the juke joint in town."

Bernard knitted his brows together. "Nalley? Jenson has been seeing her for almost two years. How's it rape?"

The noncom looked over the top of the clipboard.

Bernard had volunteered too much information. He shut his mouth and retreated.

The noncom glared at him. "I'll forget you said that or you'd be up on collusion charges." He hopped down off the truck and strode to his waiting jeep.

Souter and Higgins fell in step with Bernard on the way back to the barracks. "This could be real bad for Jenson."

Bernard waved his hand. "They'll slap him on the wrist for breaking the rules, and he'll be back in a week or two. If we're here after they get done at Normandy."

Higgins crowded close. "No, you don't understand. If they're convening a court-martial, his charges are serious."

"The girl's been going out with him for two years. How can they call it rape?"

"It depends on whether he paid her or not."

"Paid her?" Bernard spun to face them. "Are you telling me he was paying her?"

Both men nodded vigorously.

Bernard shook his head and lowered his eyes to the ground. "How bad can this get?"

24

May 8, 1945

Germany Surrenders

Cordelia's heart threatened to burst from her chest. She couldn't believe it. The quilt was finished. Her lip quivered. "Grammy, I did it," she whispered. A single tear escaped. She brushed it away and grinned. Her fingers rippled over the rows closest to her. So many prayers, and because of the loving relationship she'd developed with Anna, they were heartfelt and genuine. She'd learned much in such a short time.

She sat on the edge of the quilt where it overlapped the bed. The edging gave her pause. She had run out of old clothes and used Anna's leftover air raid curtain material. Since the landing at Normandy, the blackout requirements had stopped. Anna didn't want to waste the material, a good choice since today celebrated the German surrender. Her quilt reflected the memory. The end drew near.

Bernard would be coming home. Cordelia's very bones vibrated in anticipation. She had completed the quilt in time for their marriage bed. She lay down on the quilt, then rolled over with her hands folded underneath her chin.

"Father, thank you for protecting my precious Bernard. Thank you for your patience with me and thank you for surrounding me with people who guide me."

How different it felt to have faith in what she prayed. And like a diary, the quilt displayed the journey she had endured since Grammy started it when Cordelia was thirteen. She closed her eyes. A lifetime ago. All she'd been through made her who she was, but credit belonged to Anna, and even Bernard, for awakening her relationship with Jesus.

Why didn't any of these lessons sink in when she was a child? Why didn't she learn any of this from her preacher father? Her father . . . this was the first time she had thought of him in a while. She forgave him for what she perceived he'd done to ruin her life with Bernard. She might have been able to keep him home. Her father was deferred to because he was a family man and a preacher. But the bitterness wrapped itself around a lot of woulda, shoulda, coulda. Her forgiveness had Bernard's homecoming as a condition.

She rubbed her hand over the quilt. Soon, Bernard, soon. She could feel him slipping away in his letters. He wasn't the same. Every time she asked a question, when the next letter came, he ignored the question. He didn't seem to care. He wouldn't tell her anything about his mission over there, and none of the newspapers ever mentioned New Caledonia.

A knock interrupted her thoughts.

Cordelia raised herself and levered her legs over the side of the bed. "Yes?"

"It's Charles. Can I talk to you?"

She hopped off the bed and opened the door.

"Did you hear the news?" Charles shoved his hand into his back pocket. "The Germans have surrendered."

Cordelia smiled. "That means Bernard can come home soon. I've been praying so long for this day."

"I think you ought to be prepared. War changes a man." Charles set his jaw. "You're not going to get back the same boy who left here."

"I know," laughed Cordelia. "He's two years older."

Charles shook his head. "That's not what I mean. I've been seein' some of the fellas that came home, over at the Elks Club. They're mean and sullen, and make references to stuff people shouldn't talk about in polite society."

Cordelia cocked her head to the side. "You mean, things men shouldn't talk about in front of women?"

Charles lowered his gaze. "That, too. There's some things that womenfolk and children don't need to know."

"Are you talking about the war or your own experiences?" She did know, after numerous conversations with Charles. She understood him better.

"Both. I would never admit it to any man friend of mine, but I have you and my Anna to thank for who I've become today." Charles slumped back against the doorjamb as though a weight fell off.

"Me? What did I do?"

"Since you came here to live, I've been listenin' to you and Anna talkin' as you worked on your quilt thing at the kitchen table."

"I did notice every time we were working on it, you sat in the living room."

"I learned about forgiveness from you two. It took me a long time to understand harboring unforgiveness toward anyone or anything just takes up space in my head. It doesn't hurt them that done it to me."

Cordelia wanted to pat his hand, but she still didn't feel comfortable enough to make contact. "You've changed from the person I came to know two years ago. I think Bernard would be proud of you." She prayed for Charles daily. In fact, for a few months after their first conversation, she prayed more for Charles than she did for Bernard.

Charles shook his head. "I think there's a lot of pain between me and my son that's gonna have to be worked out before he even gets to the place where he can tolerate me. I passed on all the pain to that boy."

"I have prayed for you every day," said Cordelia. She envisioned the pain he suffered and how it demoralized him.

"I want to say thank you, but I don't think I'm worthy of God botherin' about me."

Cordelia's fingers trembled as she came in contact with his arm. "God loves you no matter what you've done. That's why he sent his Son to us. All you have to do is ask for his forgiveness, and ask the same of your son." She felt a twinge. Did she say that for Charles or herself? Was that tears she saw glistening in his eyes?

Charles turned away, his voice almost strangled. "I'll have to work up to that."

Did he mean *working up* to asking God or asking Bernard for forgiveness?

He walked quickly down the stairs.

Cordelia felt emotions well up in her for his awakening to forgiveness. It shook her reality the first time she cried for him as she prayed; after seeing his back, the depraved inhumanity of men broke her heart. The tears humbled her. Compassionate prayer snuck up on her. Grammy had told her the growth would happen, but she didn't believe. Then again, she hadn't believed in much. Now, many things Grammy prayed over were evident.

She closed her door and returned to lie on her quilt. She had her own forgiveness to work on. She wished she had listened to more of her mother's wisdom. Her old stand-by saying, *If hindsight was twenty-twenty,* made sense now. She needed to work on forgiving her parents for leaving her penniless and homeless. And she could no longer justify using Bernard's homecoming as a condition. She understood they hadn't done it on purpose, but they hadn't thought ahead either. Mom's mantra fit the situation, but they couldn't appreciate the irony now.

After quite a long time, Cordelia sat up. She traced the quilt's triangular impressions on the side of her face. Feeling the different materials, remembering the times and places attached to them, branded the emotions into her soul. "Lord, can you tell Grammy 'thank you'?"

A smile touched her lips. One of Grammy's sayings popped into her thoughts. *You'll come through the fiery furnace just like Shadrach, Meshach, and Abednego and you won't even smell like smoke.*

Cordelia slid underneath the protective weight of the quilt. Tonight would be a new beginning. Now she needed Bernard to come home and her world would be perfect and complete.

25

August 14, 1945

V-J Day

Get away from me! Haven't I told you a thousand times not to touch me when I'm sleeping?" Bernard reached over the side of his bunk and grabbed the first thing his hand came in contact with, his beer bottle from the night before. He hurled it in Souter's direction. It smashed against the footlocker at the end of Souter's bunk and disintegrated into a hundred pieces.

"I was only trying to tell you the news," said Souter. He grabbed a broom from the corner by the door and began to corral the broken glass.

Angry, Bernard rose and rubbed the sleep from his eyes. "I don't care. That's your second count. One more, and I'm going to clean your clock."

Souter bent over to scoop up the glass with the dustpan. "What was the first?"

"Short-sheeting my bunk."

"Man, it wasn't me. Higgins pulled that prank."

"Well, since I'm awake, spill it!"

"I was in the radio shack when the news came in. The Japanese have surrendered."

Bernard jumped to his feet. "Are you sure you heard it right?"

Souter grinned. "Thirty days and a wake-up, and we could be out of here."

"I won't have to see you dark ugly," said Bernard.

Higgins thrashed the sheet off and rolled over. "I won't have to see either of you sad sacks. You realize you're going to need to learn to speak English again. No one back home would know *dark ugly* means 'early in the morning.'"

"We could actually be two-digit midgets. Lord, let us have less than a hundred days left." Souter clasped his hands together in fake prayer.

Bernard looked at him. Back when he was a fresh-faced baby wipe, he would have chastised Souter for the disrespect. But truth be known, he hadn't cracked his Bible open since about six months into his tour of duty. He had slid it down in the side of his footlocker when nightmares started and the prayers weren't helping.

Bernard opened the lid and reached for the black leather Bible. He lifted it free from between his socks and undershirts.

"You screamed again last night," said Souter. He walked across the room and sat down beside Bernard. "Which was it this time? The snakes or the grenades?"

Bernard let the Bible slide back in between his clothing, and shut the lid. "I keep seeing when Stevens, from squad three, got both legs blown off."

Bernard bent over, resting his head in his hands. The image still haunted him. The legs with boots on the ends of them, smoldering where the explosion had cauterized them. One ripped a hole in the tent and landed on the table where they used to eat. No one ever ate there again.

"But you tried to help Stevens," said Souter. "Doesn't that count for something?"

Bernard looked at his bare hands and shook his head. "I see it like it happened an hour ago. The medic trying to stem the flow of blood. I bent down to help. He lifted the stump and the artery blood gushed into a jet spray soaking . . ." Bernard emitted a strangled moan, "my face and chest. I wake up seeing myself covered in it." He wiped his bare hands together and held them out to Souter. "I can't get the blood off."

Covered by the blood rolled through Bernard's mind. He shook his head and slammed a fist on the footlocker. He didn't want to think about blood.

He stormed past Souter and out of the tent.

26

September 29, 1945

Operation Magic Carpet

The pot banged. The obnoxious sound had become a nightmare for Bernard. Nothing good ever came from the annoying metal clang. What new dread would be foisted upon them today? It didn't really matter. None of it mattered. The men shuffled into the dusty area outside the mess hall.

This time it was First waiting for them in the deuce and a half. Bernard scrunched up his forehead and inhaled. First Sergeant never made ordinary announcements. The breath came out long and low like a whistle. This could be bad.

"Okay, the following men step forward on my order." He proceeded to list off most of the men in Bernard's unit. They were the ones who had been here the longest.

Souter nudged Bernard. "He called you, too. Step forward."

Bernard felt a rush of adrenaline. What could he have done wrong? He'd learned from trial and error to keep his head down and his nose clean. He searched through his last few days. He had slipped somewhere.

He stepped forward and braced for the discipline.

"Get your gear together. You're shipping out."

Bernard froze. "Where are we going, First?" He imagined some other hole in the Asian Pacific Theater worse than this one, although worse seemed impossible.

"You're all going home."

⸺⸗⸺

Morning seemed to take forever to come. Bernard's squad didn't sleep. They packed, visited men staying behind, and walked around in a daze trying to commit to memory things they had actually learned to enjoy, like raw sugar cane.

Most of the men were at the loading zone long before dawn. At seven in the morning, they loaded into a couple deuce and a halfs and traveled to the Noumea port of Grand Quay. The ride dropped them at dock number three.

Bernard stared at the water. He hadn't been to the coast since they landed in 1943. He'd sworn the next time he stood seaside he'd be headed home. He had kept the promise. It probably saved him from the trouble other guys in his platoon experienced. His chest tightened thinking about them. Men he had bunked with for two years. Men who understood him. He tamped down the pain. So many men had become brothers, and he would never see most of them again.

The *USS Elizabeth C. Stanton* was docked and ready to take them home on her return route to the West Coast after dropping off troops for the Japanese occupation. Rumor had it she had one more trip, to transport German POWs from Long Beach to Liverpool. The grand lady with five battle stars would be decommissioned in April after her last load of soldiers. Would he wake sweating and disoriented to find this exhilarating moment had become another part of his ever-going nightmare?

He mounted the ramp with the rest of his platoon. She wasn't a pretty transport. She had her share of battle scars. Different-colored steel hull panels attested to her involvement. His only desire was for her to get him home. The trip would take two weeks.

The first night at sea, a platoon from the white company barracked at the Noumea port were in a row with a squad of the Negro troops from Bernard's company. The good old boys from Jackson, Mississippi, said the soldier had slipped. The guy's squad said he was pushed. None of the facts lined up, but the end result had one of the Negro soldiers overboard and sucked in by the ship's undertow. They never set anchor to look for the body, and Bernard heard a joke about *one less of them darkies to take home.* Bernard decided to stay below deck the whole trip, as did many of his friends.

He didn't particularly like the ocean, but safety and mental preparation for a return to polite society seemed more important. At night the men discussed what to share with their families. As the ship slid through the water, the men slid into their new faces.

Younger guys like Bernard took advice from the older guys with more married experience. Bernard learned some of the things he should never talk about—like the intestinal worms they all caught from cuts and jungle sores.

No, they never experienced combat with foreign enemies. The majority of Negro soldiers spent their tours assigned to segregated supply or construction units. Other troops owned the glory of battle. Were they sent overseas to fight Nazis and Nips or to fight the white soldiers? For months after Bernard's platoon's arrival, the troops stationed in Noumea made weekly raids to his platoon's camp. Watching a bunch of Negro soldiers scatter after they threw live grenades into the camp provided entertainment. And now as a captive audience on this ship, it seemed like the program would continue.

The continual torment lasted until a direct command came down from headquarters, when it became sporadic. Several instances of lost lives only punctuated man's inhumanity to man. After one particular instance of a man in first squad losing an arm to an explosion, Bernard wet himself. Though his squad was scared, they still laughed as the wet spot traveled down the front of his fatigues. This memory joined dozens of other stories he vowed never to tell.

27

October 13, 1945

The metallic jingling of the ringing phone traveled into the kitchen. Both Charles and Anna were out of the house on errands. Cordelia wiped her wet hands on the dish towel and scooted to the phone stand.

"Hello, Howard residence," said Cordelia into the heavy black handset.

"Hey, baby. It's me."

At the sound of his voice tears spilled from her eyes. "Bernard, oh, Bernard, is it really you?" She clutched the phone as if to hold on to him. "How is this possible? Where are you?"

Bernard laughed a short snort. "Take it easy, doll face. I'm in California. Our transport docked a couple hours ago. They're putting together transport back to Fort Dix. So I'll be getting a bus home from Jersey by the end of next week."

"Oh, Bernard, I've missed you so much. I was so scared. Your letters started getting—"

"Listen, doll face, I gotta run. There's a whole line of guys behind me that wanna call home, too. See you in a week."

The phone went dead.

Cordelia stared at the receiver. Did that really just happen? Bernard is home! Her heart pounded. She hyperventilated and lurched into the coffee table, sending the lead crystal candy dish sliding off the side. Bending over to pick up the dish, she then plopped onto the couch. They both couldn't live in his bedroom. They needed an apartment.

Her heart pumped against her rib cage. They needed to get married first.

The tiny chapel belonged to a new congregation just forming in the neighborhood. Cordelia had come here for several months, and Anna had even managed to accompany her a few times. So it was the perfect place to get married.

Cordelia wore a simple white dress. Anna had lent her a delicate handmade lace collar. The white lace gloves had belonged to Cordelia's mom. It occurred to her the tradition of something old, something new, something borrowed, and something blue had not been fulfilled. She wondered if marriage success rested in the tradition. No time to worry about it now.

Bernard stood off to the side of the sanctuary. Dressed in his old Sunday suit, he presented a handsome figure of a man. But he pulled at the collar of his shirt every couple of seconds and looked ready to bolt.

Cordelia walked to his side with Anna in tow.

"You look so handsome, Son. This is a very happy day and I love you," said Anna. She touched Bernard's arm and kissed him on the cheek. She had only seen him yesterday for a few minutes when he arrived, before he announced he was very tired and needed sleep.

"I love you, too, Mom." Bernard had a pained expression on his face.

Cordelia noticed. "What's the matter?" she whispered with her back to Anna.

"I'm just nervous around this many civilians." His glance darted around the room at the dozen people assembled for the nuptials. His sweep stopped, and he let out a small groan.

Cordelia turned. Bernard's father stood in the doorway shaking hands with the reverend, who was welcoming the guests to his house of worship.

Charles looked around the room. Anna caught his attention and waved him over. Bernard groaned again.

Cordelia elbowed him in the ribs and whispered, "Stop it, and be nice. He's changed." She hadn't had an opportunity to tell Bernard about his father's progress. But she also wondered how much of it she should let the men discuss themselves if she could get them in the same room.

Charles strolled to the couple with his hands in his pockets. He looked straight at Bernard. "Welcome home, boy. I'm glad to see you made it through without injury."

Bernard stood at attention. "Thank you, sir, but injury is such a relative term."

Cordelia and Anna caught the tone right away.

Anna put her hand on Charles's arm. "Let's get to our seats so this happy event can commence."

"Yes, let's get to the front of the altar. The reverend is waiting." Cordelia led him away from his father. Charles had been at work when Bernard arrived yesterday, and this was their first encounter. Cordelia thought, *so far so good . . . maybe.*

She'd rented a three-room apartment several buildings down the Court from Anna and Charles, so their bumping into one another would be inevitable. She prayed Bernard could warm to the change in Charles and bury the pain of their past.

She strolled up the aisle on Bernard's arm. Gertie held out a small bunch of white flowers streaming with blue ribbons.

Cordelia grinned broadly and accepted them, mouthing the words *thank you.*

She continued forward to her new life.

The ceremony took all of ten minutes, and they ended surrounded by friends wishing congratulations. Cordelia wanted to introduce Bernard to Gertie's new boyfriend. Anna invited everyone to their house for sandwiches, cake, and coffee. And a couple of Bernard's old friends congratulated him for making it home.

Cordelia noticed his discomfort. He tried to pull away from the crowd several times but kept getting drawn back in by another handshake or pat on the back. His agitation grew. She decided to intervene.

"Well, Husband, what do you think?" she asked, displaying a soft smile, hoping to soothe his mood.

Bernard knit his brow. "I think I'd like to get out of here." He took Cordelia by the hand and hustled her out of the church.

Back at the apartment, Bernard stripped off the suit.

"Don't you want to go to your mom's for the reception she planned for us? Everyone else will be there."

Bernard rubbed his forehead. "I'm too tired, doll face. I've been traveling all week and I really need to rest."

"But it's our celebration."

"The only reason we got married this soon was because I didn't want you sleeping in that house another night without me."

"But your father is a perfect—"

"All I want is you," said Bernard as he wrapped his arms around her waist and kissed her long and sweet.

Cordelia ran over to Anna's to get them plates of food and cake. She expressed their regrets to the rest of the assembled group and hurried back home with a smile.

28

Cordelia held tightly to Bernard's hand as they strolled from the Laurel Line electric train, down across the grass, and into Rocky Glen Park. They followed the trail to the huge billowing tent set up near the pavilion. The October weather was uncharacteristically warm. Cordelia wiped the droplets from her forehead. Nothing could spoil her mood.

Dodging groups of laughing and playing children on the great expanse of grass made Cordelia hunger to start a family, but Bernard was dead set against it. They'd only been married a week. More unknowns lurked below the surface. He'd been withdrawn and sullen since he came home. She rarely saw any hint of the old happy Bernard.

"What do you want to do first?" She pointed toward the lake. "I want to ride on the Million Dollar Coaster!"

Bernard looked at her, not breaking a smile. "When did they put that in? Don't you think the ride is for the children?" He flinched as the coaster roared into the station landing with a great whoosh and clatter of wheels.

Cordelia grinned. "Last year. I'll still be riding the coaster when I'm fifty. I love roller coasters and the thrill of looping out over the water."

"How long do we have to stay here?" Bernard set the picnic basket on the first empty table inside the tent.

"Come on, honey, please." Cordelia ran her fingers along his arm. "Have a little fun. You're home. The war is over. We're married. Let's celebrate."

Bernard didn't look pleased in the least. He looked like he wanted to go to sleep.

Cordelia looked around and made eye contact with several of their friends. She scanned the approaching couples. "You remember Cy Williams and his girlfriend, Mandy?"

Bernard nodded at the lanky man with dirty blond hair and his petite red-headed woman.

Cordelia whispered, "They got married last year, and she just had a baby. It's not fat, it's leftover baby." The woman wore a maternity top. It covered her almost to the bottom of her shorts.

She leaned into his ear as he seated himself on the long bench seat. "And you know Gertie. She's with her new man, Jake. He was in the Navy."

Bernard stood and shook hands with Jake as they exchanged service info.

Cordelia relaxed. Finally, someone he could identify with. But both men sat down and the conversation petered out.

"Cordelia, are you still going to buy the car abandoned at Stoney's?" Mandy pulled plates and silverware from her basket as Cordelia did the same.

She smiled. "Well, I would if he could ever get it running. Since Bernard is home, I'm sure it can be fixed." She sat beside him and wrapped her arms around his elbow.

Cy Williams popped the cap from his pop bottle by rapping it on the edge of the picnic table. Soda splashed on his loose-fitting summer shirt. He brushed it away. "How's it feel being home, Bernard?" Cordelia lamented that he had been ineligible for service because of his flat feet. Why couldn't Bernard have had fallen arches?

Bernard looked at Cy for a few seconds, then lowered his head. "Fine."

Cy laughed. "Is that all you have to say after being away for two years?"

Bernard raised his head, and a steel façade rolled over his countenance. "Is there some other answer you're looking for?" Cy pulled his chin back. "Uh, no, sorry, man. I meant no disrespect."

Bernard's eyes bayoneted Cy. "None taken."

Cordelia watched the exchange. She rubbed Bernard's back and smiled. His touchiness about basically nothing bothered her. This hadn't been the first time he'd been intentionally rude to someone who tried to make polite conversation. What was going on with him?

The ladies finished setting the table as they jabbered away about the late October heat and new shoes. Both subjects passed over the men's heads. Cy and Jake discussed baseball while Bernard looked off toward the lake.

An automobile pulled into the parking lot two buildings over from the pavilion and backfired with a resounding boom. The people seated around Cordelia flinched. The ladies giggled as they each lowered their hands from their chests. Cordelia noticed the solemn look on Jake's face and followed his gaze to her right.

Bernard was not beside her.

Cordelia noticed his shoe sticking out from under the table. She bent. Bernard sat under the table trembling, knees pulled to his chest, hands clutching the top of his head with his elbows protecting his face.

Jake set his jaw and grimaced. His voice remained steady as he walked around the table. "It was a car backfiring. It's all right, Bernard. Let me help you." He reached out a hand.

Bernard slapped it away.

Cordelia moved the bench, and he crawled out from her side of the table. Sweat beaded his forehead.

Cordelia touched his arm. He pushed it away and turned from the group. He stood in military at ease, hands against the back of his hips.

Jake raised a hand to silence the ladies. "Why don't you girls take a trip to the Fun House or the Ferris wheel and let us men talk."

The women looked at each other and shrugged their shoulders. Cordelia rose from her seat. "Bernard," she said softly as she touched his shoulder. He flinched. She drew back her hand. "I'll be back in a little while."

"Yeah," said Bernard without turning to her as she backed away from the table.

Cordelia, Gertie, and Mandy strolled across the fairway. Gertie bought them each a cotton candy. Cordelia splurged for the soda pop, all the while keeping her eye on the men talking.

"Come on," said Mandy. "I want to ride the Ferris wheel."

Cordelia loved roller coasters but traveling around in a circle made her nauseous. "You girls go right ahead," she said, and then took a swig of her ice-cold Royal Crown Cola.

The girls walked off. Cordelia leaned against the food counter watching Jake talk to Bernard. They had an animated conversation for about ten minutes, then Bernard jumped to his feet and stormed off toward the lake.

Cordelia ran after him.

Jake intercepted her. "Let him go."

Cordelia tried to push by him. "Why? Bernard looks upset. He needs me."

"No, he doesn't need you right now. He needs you to understand him."

"What are you talking about? He's my husband. I understand him." She wondered how true that statement was at this point.

"Bernard is suffering from what we call battle fatigue," said Jake. His expression turned grave.

"But he wasn't in any battles. He was at a supply depot in the South Pacific."

"The kind of combat Bernard saw was just as debilitating, and he suffered very harsh conditions."

"So how long will it take him to get over it? Will he be all right in a week, a month, a year?"

Jake shook his head.

Bernard came back from the concession stand with a bottle of beer in his hand before she could ask more questions.

Bernard's behavior appalled Cordelia. Bernard had never drunk alcohol before he left home. Bernard, with a beer, would have sent her father on an unending rant. For the rest of the picnic, Bernard wasn't nervous or agitated—because he was drunk.

———

Cordelia folded back the quilt and laid it on the cedar chest. Her hands rested on the heavy, multidimensional creation. This was her covering, her security, and her prayers and dreams. But now it belonged to both of them. Every word she'd ever spoken over him wove through this tapestry of colors. She'd spent two years praying for him to come home to her and the Lord had honored her prayers. But this bent and broken man didn't resemble the full-of-life boy who left here two years ago.

Cordelia slumped to the bed. Heaven help her. What was she going to do? He wouldn't go back to church. The only time he'd been in the building since he returned was for their wedding, and he had hurried her out of the sanctuary so fast she almost lost a shoe.

She rested her head on the quilt. She needed to talk to Jake again. After church? She had to understand. *Lord, give me strength. Help me get my Bernard back. Help me understand all this.*

As she prayed, Bernard came out of the bathroom. She slid off the bed and turned back the covers.

He staggered into the bedroom, gripping the doorjamb.

Cordelia smiled. "Honey, are you feeling better now?"

Bernard mumbled something, then cleared his throat. "Why do we need this stupid quilt on the bed? It's too hot."

"It will cool off during the night, and I don't like to wake up cold." A shiver coursed through her. She wasn't cold. Grammy often said shivers were someone walking over your grave. Cordelia dismissed the nonsensical thought.

He waved her off and tumbled into bed.

"But if it—"

He rolled away from her and pulled the covers to his ears.

Cordelia's bottom lip quivered. How could things go this terribly wrong? She had dreamed for years of being his wife, lying in their marriage bed, and now it was a ravaged, loveless place. She just wanted him to hold her.

"Bernard." She touched his back.

"What?" He rolled over. "I need to get some sleep. It's been a hard day." He jerked back in the other direction and yanked the covers over his head.

A tear escaped. She rubbed it away with the back of her hand. No crying. I'm stronger than this. It'll blow over and things will get back to normal as soon as he finds a job. She thought about quitting the factory, but at the moment they needed the money.

———oxxo———

Pounding blows slammed into the side of her face. Cordelia jerked awake and screamed. The quilt, over her head, shielded her from the full force of the pounding. She raised her hands to ward off the rapid hits. Her arms were struck repeatedly. Sharp pain shot to her shoulder.

"Bernard, help," she screamed, now with both arms and legs flailing. Who was attacking them? She fought her way from under the quilt. Bernard was on his knees above her.

Cordelia propelled herself off her side of the bed and onto the floor with a resounding thud. Her hips smarted from the hard fall.

He kept beating on the quilt. He groaned while a thread of spittle hung from his mouth. His eyes were open but not focused. She screamed again. The pounding intensified.

Cordelia scrambled from the floor. She could feel her lip swelling, and her eye hurt. "Bernard, stop!" she screamed.

He didn't hear her. He remained fixated.

"Bernard!" No answer.

Cordelia took a deep breath and lunged at him with both hands. She connected with his shoulders, throwing him off the bed on the other side. She landed on top of the quilt and bounced before coming to rest hanging over the side of the bed.

Bernard lay sprawled out on the floor. His hand went to his head. "What am I doing on the floor?" His head jerked in several directions as he looked around the room.

Cordelia shook from the drama. "Do you know where you are?"

190

Bernard rubbed his head. "Of course I know where I am." He stood up. "Do you think I'm stupid?"

Cordelia backed off the bed. She rubbed her mouth.

Bernard looked at her. "What happened to your mouth? It's swollen."

"You hit me." Cordelia's knees buckled. The bed broke her fall.

Bernard stumbled to his side of the bed. He reached out to touch her face.

She flinched and turned away.

"I'm sorry," said Bernard in a thick, anguished tone. "I didn't know. I thought I was fighting the snake."

Cordelia lowered her hand and turned back to face him. "The snake?"

Bernard's hands started to shake. His eyes blinked rapidly and his mouth contorted in pain. "I can't. I can't talk about it." He bolted from the bed, grabbed his pillow, and dashed for the bathroom.

The door slammed behind him.

29

The tinny jangling of the alarm jolted Cordelia awake. She squinted with the sunshine pouring in through the thin curtains. She groped the nightstand for the offending clock. The circular metal beast vibrated out of reach. She pushed onto one elbow and snatched the escaping timepiece before it teetered over the edge. She flicked the off button, and her head slumped back to the pillow as her eyelids sagged.

Was it all a dream? As the fog receded, pain inched in to claim its place. A twinge pulled at the corner of her eye. Her right elbow hurt. She raised her arm to inspect it and saw an angry black and blue oval that spread across her forearm, enveloping her elbow. She gasped, but the movement of her mouth met resistance.

Cordelia squeezed her eyes shut. How could this happen? Everything she had feared her entire life had just been dealt to her in one swift blow. She might have been right all along. She must be unworthy—even Bernard had turned on her. Did she deserve it? She must not be a good wife, or Bernard would be happy. He'd given much for his country, yet she continued to make him angry. No one had ever taught her how to act for a husband. When she was a bad child, she got switched. Did she deserve to be beaten? Is this what happened to bad wives?

She clutched at the quilt. *Jesus, help me. How do I fix this?* Who could she ask? She never heard other women at the factory talk about this kind of problem. Family business. She'd been taught her entire life to keep home matters private. She couldn't talk about it.

Her head tipped to the side, remembering the horror. It ended with the same statement. Bernard said he couldn't talk about it. Talk about what? Was he still in the bathroom or had he deserted her after she fell asleep?

She pulled the quilt close. There had to be someone. Gertie? If she told her, Bernard might be in trouble. Gertie didn't play around with men who were physical. She might try to poke him in the nose.

She threw back the covers and cringed in pain. He'd hit her. It wasn't her imagination. Every part of her body hurt at the moment.

No! Run away. Her mind raced through an escape plan, but her fingers clutched the material in her hand.

Cordelia stopped. She looked down at the fabric. *This is your life cover* rolled through her mind. Grammy might have known, but surely God knew this moment was coming. Why had he put her here? Did he love her? Her throat tightened. She raised her chin. In her mind, she could hear Grammy telling her to get on her knees.

Cordelia slid from the bed, drew the quilt with her, and wrapped up in it as her knees made contact with the floor. She leaned her head against the bed. "Lord, help me," she repeated over and over.

She prayed, and cried, and prayed some more. The pain, the fear, and her dashed dreams all ran together. She had wanted this life forever. Stupid. Childish dreams never turned into reality. She'd dreamed of Grammy being at her wedding. She'd dreamed of her parents being grandparents to her children. None of it had worked out. She had never contemplated what would happen if it didn't work out. She glanced at the clock and panicked.

Half an hour before she was due at work—the time included running the two blocks to get there. She couldn't afford to get fired now. Throwing the quilt onto the bed, she grabbed coveralls and a long-sleeved shirt. No time for anything cute or fancy.

She ran for the bathroom and threw open the door, momentarily forgetting that Bernard had taken refuge in there. Cordelia slid to a stop. He slept curled in the fetal position in the bathtub. Her mind jumbled. He looked innocent and deceptively docile.

But she knew better. One more life lesson she had learned that would never be forgotten.

Cordelia tiptoed to the sink, ran a little water to wash her face and brush her teeth, then scooted from the room. She leaned against the closed door. The night replayed in her head, but she shook it off. No time now. She had to protect her job.

A stirring noise and a grunt came from the bathroom. He could open the door, and it might start all over again. Dressing quickly, she smoothed out the bedclothes and spread the quilt flat. Was she crazy? Why worry about the bed, when Bernard and losing her job were the more critical problems? Maybe it was just to have some semblance of control at this crazy moment. She rushed out the front door. At least she had begun her morning without another conflict.

The humid morning air assaulted her lungs. It was like inhaling mud. Would it ever get seasonably cold? Cordelia gasped for air as she charged down the alley. Layoffs had affected too many since the war ended. She worked vigorously to save her own job. Now was not the time to be late.

She rushed in the front door of the factory as the morning bell sounded. Sewing machines across the factory floor roared into action. Cordelia slipped into her chair. All eyes had followed her to her seat.

"What are you looking at?" She hadn't stopped to brush her hair. She smoothed it down until she could take a break and get to the bathroom. A twinge pulled at her elbow.

Sitting at the machine next to her, Gertie stared at Cordelia's bruises. "Cordelia! What happened to your face?"

Cordelia grabbed a bundle of pant legs, untied the cord, and spread the bundle from the work bin to her machine. "I don't know what you're talking about." If she ignored what had happened, there would be no truth to it.

Gertie ran her tongue around the inside of her cheek, reached down beside her, and pulled a compact from her purse. With a flourish, she flipped open the lid and shoved it in Cordelia's direction.

She accepted the Bakelite case and held it to her face. Cordelia saw her own horrified expression.

Black, blue, and purple bruises snaked from her hairline down to her jaw, and her bottom lip looked like a tire pump had filled it with air. Cordelia scrambled from her chair and ran to the bathroom. The shop steward yelled for her to come back to her seat, but she kept going.

Cordelia dabbed a moistened wad of toilet paper to her face, as though the bruises would wipe off. Touching them made the bruises hurt worse. She stared at the mess in the large mirror over the row of sinks. How had it come to this?

Gertie peeked in. "Mind if I come in?"

"There's no sense saying no. You'd come in anyhow," said Cordelia as she threw the toilet paper in the trash can and leaned back against the sink.

"You wanna tell me how this happened?" Gertie jammed her hands in her pockets.

Cordelia shook her head then, looked down. "It was an accident. I really don't want to talk about it."

"I've seen automobile crashes with a lot less damage. This was no accident. What gives?"

Cordelia bit down on her lip and yelped in pain. "I don't know what happened."

Gertie grabbed her by the shoulders. Cordelia whimpered and lifted Gertie's hand off her right arm. Gertie pushed up Cordelia's sleeve, then released a long, low whistle. "We've got enough black and blue going on here to polish a pair of shoes. You sticking with your I-don't-know story?"

Cordelia covered her face with both hands. Her thoughts of a happy life were evaporating. "Please, just let it go."

The door to the ladies' room opened, and Mary Walker stuck her head in. "Vinnie is hopping mad. You two need to get to your machines while you still have jobs."

30

Cordelia eased into the line crowding around the time clock. She struggled to walk without a limp. The ache in her hip had settled and stiffened from sitting at her machine all day. Falling off the bed last night had also wrenched the base of her spine. Grammy's old lady aches and pains made sense now.

Gertie caught up as Cordelia punched her card. "Okay, now that we're getting out of here, we need to talk."

"What else can I say other than let it go?" Cordelia punched the button to stamp her card and slid it into an outgoing slot. She hurried out the double doors, with Gertie right behind her.

"Girlfriend, it's been you and me together for a couple years now, and you can bet your sweet patootie I know when you're hiding something. Your face gives you away." She glanced across Cordelia's bruised face, then grimaced. "That wasn't exactly what I meant."

Cordelia hitched a half smile. At least the swelling in her lip had gone down. "I know what you meant." She walked Gertie away from the doors and leaned against one of the picnic tables. "I just don't know what to say. Bernard's having a real hard time being home. He's nervous and touchy half the time, and sullen and withdrawn the rest."

"It will probably just take time for him to get used to being home, and you having a job." Gertie pursed her lips. "Nah, what am I saying? I don't even believe that line. He doesn't have the right to be putting his hands on you."

"I was talking to Jake at the picnic, and he said Bernard is suffering from battle fatigue."

"How do you fix it?"

"I don't know. He said it would take time. But if Bernard went back to work, it might help him start feeling normal."

"Has he had any luck finding work?" Gertie glanced at the people exiting the factory.

"No, Stoney replaced him, and the guy is fighting to hang onto his job."

"Why don't you ask Vinnie if he needs another machine mechanic or something?"

"I don't think it's a good idea." Cordelia feared the way Bernard might act if he heard the shop steward yelling at her. She'd learned to deal with her boss, but Bernard . . . he seemed as though he . . . well, he needed a rest for a while. Besides, she didn't want Bernard and his father in close proximity to one another on a regular basis until the mental wounds had started to heal.

Gertie motioned to Vinnie as he came out of the building.

"No, don't say anything," said Cordelia, but it was too late.

Vinnie sauntered over to them.

"You two ladies need to pick up the pace and stop spending time in the bathroom gabbing." With a sly smile, Vinnie looked Cordelia over while ignoring Gertie. "I can replace you easy as pie, if you don't produce the goods."

Cordelia squirmed. She didn't like it when he leered at her, but she knew how to handle his advances.

"Cordelia's husband is home from the war, and he needs a job," said Gertie, her hands propped on her ample hips.

Vinnie lowered his chin and looked over the top of his glasses at Gertie. "What are you, her husband's agent? Cordelia can speak for herself," said Vinnie. "Or maybe the fat lip she had this morning is restricting her conversation."

Cordelia planted her feet as though she was ready to fight. She pointed at him. "Listen, Vinnie, it's none of your business."

"What's going on here?"

Cordelia wheeled to find Bernard, unshaven and less than pleasant, with a slight aroma of beer about him. She frowned and put herself between Vinnie and her husband. "Nothing, nothing at all. We were arguing about baseball."

She attempted to take Bernard by the hands and turn him toward the road. He resisted and moved her out of the way. "Oh, really? It looked to me like this here guy was being rude." With a cold and stony expression, he faced Vinnie. "Were you being rude to my wife?"

Vinnie glared. The hint of a grin played at the corner of his mouth. "This must be the war hero come home to fight—"

"Okay, we have to go now," said Cordelia, taking Bernard by the hand. She pulled him in the opposite direction.

Bernard pushed her hand away. "I want to hear him out. I think he needs an education." His fist balled.

Cordelia pressed in close to him and spoke in a low voice, "Please, he's my boss. Don't start anything. I need the job right now until you find work."

His nostrils flared. The realization he needed his wife's money seemed to enrage Bernard. He grabbed Cordelia's hand and stormed out of the alley to the road.

—∞∞∞—

Cordelia let him lead her home. Actually, he dragged her home, but he held her hand the whole time, and it felt good to her. She'd wait until they were behind closed doors before she spoke.

Bernard let go of her hand to shove open the front door to their tiny apartment.

Cordelia looked down the alley. His parent's house was only six doors away, yet she could count on one hand the number of times he'd visited since he'd been home. She ached for Anna. She knew the woman missed her son.

"I'm glad to see you went outside today. Did you have any luck applying for a job?" Cordelia took potatoes and onions from the bin to start dinner. Grammy always said the way to a man's heart was through his stomach. Maybe good home cooking would help.

Bernard walked past her to the bedroom, ignoring the question. She followed him, noticing several beer bottles on the coffee table. Her heart sank.

"How about coming to the new church with me on Sunday? You'd like the reverend if you'd give him a chance."

Bernard plopped onto the bed and spread out on the quilt with his shoes on. Cordelia winced at the thought of shoe dirt on the quilt but decided it might be better to keep her opinion to herself.

"No, I'm not interested in going to church. I've had enough of God to last me a lifetime," said Bernard. He clasped his hands behind his head.

"I don't understand."

"What is there to not understand? I'm done with God. How many other ways do you want me to say it?"

Her lip quivered. "How can you say you're done with God? What happened to you over there?"

Bernard ground his shoes into the quilt and rolled onto his side.

She couldn't take it anymore. He was going to ruin the quilt. "Please, let me take your shoes off." She reached for his feet.

He pulled his feet from her reach, bunching the quilt.

She grabbed for the quilt. "Your shoes are going to get the quilt all dirty. Please let me take them off." She reached out again.

He pulled back again, this time visibly angry. "What is your problem? It's a stupid quilt. Put it in the wash if it gets dirty."

"It's not a stupid quilt." Her eyes teared. "This is what got you home to me."

"Are you crazy?" He shot up straight. "I'm what got me home to you, not some piece of material." He snatched the quilt. "You, and the way you go on about this stupid thing, are getting on my nerves."

He wrapped both hands in the fabric at the edge of the quilt and tried to rip it in half.

"No!" screamed Cordelia. She lunged over the bed on all fours to reach his hands. "Don't! Let it go!" She clawed at his hands, raking her nails along his arm, desperate to rescue the quilt.

He twisted out of her reach, looked down at the deep scratch on his forearm, and brought the red streak to his mouth to lick off the blood. "You've turned into quite a scrapper. You're not the sweet, docile girl I left behind."

Cordelia clenched the quilt in her arms and backed away from the bed. "And you're not the loving man I kissed goodbye at the bus station."

Bernard wiped his arm on his pant leg. "War changes people."

"I understand, but you're home now, and it's over."

"Do you really think it's that easy?" He snapped his fingers. "Poof! The war is over. Forget everything that happened and just get back to normal."

Cordelia wrinkled her forehead. "Well, yes, it's all gone now."

Bernard's face contorted. "It will *never* be gone. I will never forget, and there is no more normal."

"How about God? God is the same yesterday, today, and tomorrow."

"I don't believe in God anymore."

Cordelia recoiled. "That's ridiculous. You were raised in the church. You've known Jesus your entire life. How can you not believe in God anymore?"

Bernard turned away from her. His shoulders hunched. He emitted a strangled cry and punched a hole in the wallboard. His hand remained against the hole as though it were being held. "Because he deserted me when I needed him most."

Cordelia stepped forward, then hesitated. He was in a bad way again. "God would never desert you. Why do you think that?"

Bernard whipped around.

She stumbled back at his rage.

His mouth opened, then closed. He shut his eyes and clamped his lips. "Leave me alone. Please, leave me alone. I'm no good for you."

He pulled his hand from the wall, shaking his head. "I'm broken. We're all broken. I need to go away." He moved to the closet.

Cordelia ran to him. "No, you can't go. You can't leave me!"

He ignored her, and rummaged in the closet for his duffle bag.

She wanted to argue, but fear strangled her vocal cords. All she could manage was a cry. "Bernard!"

He ignored her. Throwing the bag on the floor, he pulled open drawers and threw clothes toward the bag.

Cordelia grabbed the clothes. "I said no! You're not leaving me!" She threw the clothes back in the open drawer.

He pushed her out of the way and tossed the jumble back to the floor.

Cordelia snatched them again, and stomped on the bag. "I love you, and you're not leaving. Do you hear me?"

He ignored her and moved to the bathroom for his shaving kit.

Cordelia blocked the door. He moved to step around her, but she wrapped her arms around his neck and cried. He tried to disengage her, but she hung on for dear life. They tussled back and forth. He finally broke down. The fight went out of him, and he sank to the floor with her still holding on.

"I love you. Please don't leave me. I'll die without you," cried Cordelia.

Bernard cried. "You may die with me. I'm broken. I don't know how to fix it."

"We need God to help us."

"God deserted me. I haven't talked to him in a long time."

"God didn't desert you. He watched over you and brought you home to me," said Cordelia. She stroked Bernard's face and wiped the tears from his cheeks.

His shoulders slumped. He buried his head in her chest and cried.

31

November, 1945

November put an end to the colorful display of red, yellow, and orange fall foliage. Cordelia and Anna spent many hours at the farmers market, and even more time canning their bounty for the coming winter. With a light heart, Cordelia stocked their pantry shelves to high heaven. They'd eat well this winter.

Anna carried the last of her tomato jars into the pantry, while Cordelia loaded six quart jars into her basket, a napkin between each jar to avoid breaking them. "I'll come down and get the rest of the jars after dinner, Mom."

"All right, sweetheart. I'll give you a couple more jars of Bernard's favorite peaches." Anna folded the dish towels on which they'd placed the jars to cool.

"Wonderful " said Cordelia. "I'll take one with me. He can have them after dinner. I know it will make him happy."

"Come have a cup of coffee with me before you go," said Anna as she brought cups and saucers to the table. "Tell me how he's coping with being home."

Cordelia seated herself at the table and stirred a little milk into her cup. "He has his moments. The nightmares are still terrible, but I've learned to sleep light and get out of the way of his thrashing." She shook her head. "He's tormented. But he won't talk about it yet. It grieves my heart that I can't help him."

Anna reached over and patted her hand. "My sweet girl, you are more than I could have possibly prayed for my precious Bernard. You're a saint."

"No, I wouldn't go that far. I love him and I'll fight to get him back from whatever evil has a claim on him."

"Has he talked about going back to church yet?" Anna lifted her cup and blew across the surface of the hot liquid.

When Cordelia's father took Bernard's job from him, Anna struggled with church. But earlier this year she joined the small church where Cordelia and Bernard got married. So far, she was enjoying the weekly ministering of the Word.

"I haven't figured out how to solve that problem yet. First, I have to get him away from those other soldiers at the Lodge. He's taken to spending his days over there drinking."

Anna waved a hand. "I can't believe my child turned his back on God and is carousing with those wild boys."

"I keep praying. Something bad must have happened. I can't get him to talk."

"It's ironic that Bernard helped me find my way back to the Lord, and now he is lost. I wish he'd let me help him." Cordelia finished her coffee. "I've tried to get him down here, but he doesn't want to have much to do with Charles. He always held it against him for the way you were treated."

"But I've forgiven Charles. He's a different man now that all the badness came out in the open. Does Bernard know about it?"

"No, I didn't feel it was my place to tell him. Besides, it would open other old wounds better left alone for the time being. I guess I was waiting for him to want to meet with his father, and let them work it out." Cordelia placed the cup back on the porcelain saucer.

"Well, then, it's going to have to be you, my sweet, who brings him back to the Lord."

Cordelia rubbed her forehead. "That's a tall order. I prayed him home, and I intend to pray him through this. I need to ask Jake's advice about a few more things."

Anna looked at her. "You mean Melba Kendall's good-looking boy who was in the Navy?"

"Yes, he gave me good advice at the picnic last month." She had managed to get through a whole month of Bernard with no adverse effects.

32

Cordelia lugged her basket down the alley and into their tiny apartment. Someday soon Bernard would find a job and life would get better. She wanted children. Life had to get better.

Bernard was not there. She glanced at the clock. Four o'clock on Saturday afternoon. Her stomach went into its familiar knot. He was going to come in stumbling drunk any minute. He'd added fits of cursing to his repertoire. Rather than abate, his anger grew. If only she understood the reasons for his pain. She spent a lot of time in prayer asking the Lord to give her the strength and wisdom, but her stamina was flagging.

A shuffling on the narrow porch, then the doorknob rattled. Cordelia steeled herself. She reached for the knob as Bernard stumbled in.

"Honey, dinner will be ready in a half hour. Your mom sent you some of her canned peaches." She pasted a smile on her face. "Let me help you."

"Don't need no help." His speech was slurred, and spittle formed in the corner of his mouth. Bernard's hand chopped at the air erratically as he staggered forward and caught his balance on the kitchen table. He lurched toward the living room.

"I'll start the food. You need to get something in your stomach."

"Don't want food. Sleep." He zigzagged through the living room and into the bedroom. She heard the springs squeak as he collapsed onto the bed.

Cordelia sat at the kitchen table and put her head in her hands. "Lord, help me. How do I get through to him?" Alcohol was clearly a very difficult demon to fight. Feelings of defeat overwhelmed her, but she couldn't give up. Wouldn't give up.

There was no sense starting dinner until he actually woke. She could get her potatoes and onions peeled and into a pot of water. She busied herself with prep work to keep her mind off her sense of hopelessness, but continued a silent conversation with the Lord. Time wandered by, and the next time she looked at the clock it was five-fifteen.

Bernard's scream vibrated through the house.

Cordelia dropped her paring knife. It clattered against the colander and into the sink.

Another scream.

Her knees wobbled. She darted to the bedroom, where Bernard thrashed about on the bed. He'd rolled himself in the quilt and fought to get free.

Cordelia reached over him and untangled the leading edge of the quilt. As she pulled it back, Bernard flailed out with his right hand balled into a fist. Cordelia ducked, but he caught her square in the left cheek. The spot turned warm and tears welled in her eyes. She refused to back away.

"Bernard," she yelled. She blinked back the tears and pushed away from another direct blow.

Shouting didn't get his attention. She shoved at his hip. "Wake up!" She pushed again.

Bernard bolted off the bed, arms and legs swinging in all directions.

Cordelia backed away as he hit the floor. Had he hurt himself? She rushed toward him, then stumbled back out of the way when his fist slammed into the nightstand. His eyes flew open and curse words rolled off his tongue as easily as he spoke when sober.

She barely recognized the person he had become, but she was determined to fight for him. Her prayers were not wasted. God had prepared her for this. Her time with Anna had given her the fortitude to overcome the evil trying to claim the man she loved. She stood her ground.

Finally he rolled into the fetal position with his head and knees partially under the bed. He rocked.

Cordelia knelt beside him. Her heart ached to comfort him. She gently rubbed his back. For a moment, his body relaxed, then he stiffened and sat up.

Bernard's eyes opened. "Cordelia . . . what are you doing here?"

Cordelia tipped her head. "What do you mean? This is our bedroom."

His eyes glanced around as the realization hit. "I'm home?"

His knees were pulled to his chest and he wrapped his arms tightly around them. He hung his head and rocked back and forth several times. "I'm no good for you. I need to leave."

Her heart sank. *We're back to this again.* "Why do you think you need to leave?"

"Because . . . I'm going to hurt you again."

"How can you say that? Don't you love me?"

His head jerked. "Yes, I love you with all my heart. But I can't control this."

"Bernard, please help me understand. I don't want to lose you."

"Returning soldiers at the Elks talk about their wives leaving and divorcing them. One guy is in prison for killing his wife."

Cordelia recoiled. "He killed his wife! Why did it happen?"

Bernard emitted one of those strangled cries again. "He didn't mean it. It was an accident. It wasn't her he was killing. It was a Japanese soldier." He pulled Cordelia to him by the waist. "I don't want to ever hurt you again." He buried his head in her arms.

Tears slid down her face as she wrapped her arms around him. "I'm not leaving you. You have been my whole world since the day we met."

Cordelia and Bernard sat on the bed, arms locked around one another for almost a half hour. Cordelia's spirit soared. The close and tender warmth, from his body and soul, gave her renewed hope. The floodgates opened. Bernard poured out his heart. They cried together until no tears were left. His posture relaxed for the first time since he came home.

"We're supposed to be together. Grammy promised me," said Cordelia, wiping the tears from her face.

Bernard lifted his head, a pained expression on his face. "How could she promise we'd be together?"

Cordelia stood. Her hands reached out to the bed and smoothed out the quilt, to make it lay flat. She pulled Bernard to his feet. "Do you see this? This is our life together, in prayers."

Bernard staggered slightly. "You talking about this quilt again?"

"Come here. Sit with me." She drew him to the edge of the bed. "Do you see this red material near the center? Do you know where it came from?"

Bernard squinted, rubbing the back of one hand across his eyes. "No, it's just red material."

"It was the material from the shirt you threw away the day we met. Remember you didn't want your parents to know you'd been fighting again?"

Bernard's eyes lit as the recollection dawned. "Are you telling me you saved it?"

Cordelia smiled and nodded. "That and quite a few others." She pointed out numerous pieces made of clothing belonging to him.

A genuine smile lifted his lips. He pointed at a dark shade of blue. "You little sneak. I wondered where that shirt went. I always thought my mom got rid of it, just to get me out of it."

Cordelia giggled. "Believe me, it was my thought the day I snatched it while you were playing basketball."

Bernard rubbed his chin as he eyed each different color in the quilt. "What does all of this mean? Besides showing me how light-fingered you were?"

"Grammy taught me to pray. She prayed for me too." Cordelia turned to him. "And she prayed for you, too. This is my life covering. For a long time I had my own doubts, but this is all the hopes, dreams, and prayers for my life. Grammy said if I took care of my quilt, it would take care of me. You've always been a part of it." She touched his cheek. "This represents all the prayers I said for you while you were gone so you would come home safe."

Bernard set his jaw. "I came home . . . but not safe."

Cordelia leaned in and put her head on his shoulder. "Tell me please what has hurt you this much."

Bernard still appeared a little tipsy. She hoped tipsy enough to loosen his tongue and let him talk to her without the inhibitions always between them.

She played with the fingers of his hand that was resting on his lap. "Talk to me. Tell me how to help you. I love you."

Bernard shook his head.

She could see the wall creeping back. She touched his face.

He took her hand from his cheek and kissed her palm, then pressed her hand back to his face.

"I just need to know what we're dealing with."

Bernard turned to face her straight on. "This isn't your burden. It's mine."

"But we are one now. We're married."

Bernard turned away. She was losing ground again. She softened her voice. "Try to tell me how you feel. Please. I won't berate you."

He didn't turn back.

"I don't even know how to explain." He shook his head again. "I can't enjoy myself sitting in public. I feel like everyone is staring at me. What are they staring at me for? Is something wrong? Are they plotting something? It's these crazy thoughts in my head."

At last! Cordelia remembered what Jake had said about battle fatigue. "You're home and safe."

"It doesn't matter what you think. I can't sit without having my back against the wall because I feel threatened."

Cordelia winced. She remembered how uncomfortable he had been at the picnic, out in the open. "I'm sorry." Her words rang shallow and irrelevant. She was afraid to say too much and shut him down again.

"You're sorry? I'm the one who sees danger in every moment of every day. My brain races all the time." He put his head down again. "Sometimes I think I'd be better off dead."

Cordelia froze. "No, don't think like that."

His eyes widened. "You have no idea how many nights I wake up thinking somebody's throwing grenades at me or those pieces of . . . the weapons we got, misfired."

What could she say about war? She didn't have any reference points.

His expression saddened. "I wondered if I was over there to fight the Japanese or our white soldiers."

"Our white soldiers? Why would you say that? What happened?"

"We were segregated the whole war."

"It doesn't make sense. Did you misunderstand?"

His face hardened. "There was nothing to misunderstand."

"Did the other men feel the same way? Like Howie? Wasn't he the preacher's kid from New Jersey? What did he have to say?"

Bernard's eyes welled with tears. He put his head down on the quilt. Cordelia leaned closer. "What's the matter? What did I say?' She replayed her words.

She could see his struggle. He had to get it out. She stroked his shoulder. "Tell me, please."

At first, he whispered.

She strained to hear. "I . . . I couldn't hear you."

He cleared his throat and rose, straightening his back. Bernard suddenly looked a hundred years old, as though all the pain had settled into his face. "They hung him."

Cordelia recoiled as though she'd been slapped in the face. "Who? What are you talking about?"

Bernard's voice came out small and frail. "You asked about Howie." Tears flowed down his face in tiny rivers, dripping onto his arms and soaking into the quilt. "God forgive me for not taking it serious at the time. They hung him."

Cordelia grabbed his arm. "Who hung him?"

"Our military. There was a tribunal. He and three other soldiers were accused of raping a Red Cross worker."

Bernard's grief made Cordelia shiver.

He pounded his fist into his thigh.

Cordelia covered his fist with her hand.

The rage slowly subsided.

"I can't believe he'd do that. Not from what you told me of him." She began to understand his helplessness.

"The woman lied." Bernard bared his teeth and stabbed a finger at the air. Anger poured from him, frightening Cordelia. "She'd been shacking up with all of them on a regular basis. Howie joked he was just about paying her full rent for all she charged him. She got caught fraternizing by one of the locals and she yelled rape."

"But couldn't he have a lawyer, or you guys to testify for him?"

"They didn't believe none of us. They distributed a document about rape with pictures of nooses and assaulted women. It demoralized the Southern guys, but I didn't take it serious. I didn't think . . ."

Cordelia sat speechless. She had heard rumors of military segregation. Many others said it couldn't possibly be that bad. The more men came home, the more it sank in. What could she say? "I'm sorry."

Bernard hugged her to him. "God deserted us."

"No, God would never desert you. I don't believe it."

"Then why did he let those bad things happen? Let Howie die?"

"Bernard, you know. Think! You studied the Bible for your whole life. Bad things happen to good people!" She could barely breathe, but she didn't want to break the moment.

"It was different when it happened to me. I lost faith real fast. I felt abandoned and hopeless. Morale fell so low, if the war hadn't ended when it did, there'd have been more than one of us who ended our lives."

Cordelia said a silent thank-you to the Lord. "It's how it is in this world. The enemy is always ready to jump on any chink in our God-armor and destroy us."

"I feel like a hypocrite," said Bernard. "I fell far from God. I don't know if I can ever find my way back."

"But God never left you. He brought you back home to me. We can get through this together." Cordelia smiled. "Grammy said."

Bernard raised the corners of his mouth. "Your Grammy said, huh? Did she tell you how we were going to survive until I got a job? I heard the guys talking about women getting laid off to help returning soldiers get their jobs." He lay across the bed with arms outstretched.

"God will provide," said Cordelia. She rubbed his back and said a silent prayer of thanks for their breakthrough. At least she had some understanding of his pain now. Her job was to learn how to talk him through this and back to God.

Bernard fondled the pieces of quilt made from clothing he hadn't seen since he was a child. "What are the lumps for?"

Cordelia stopped rubbing and glanced around at his face. "What are you talking about?"

Bernard leaned on one elbow. "I asked what these lumps are for." He held one of the spots between his thumb and forefinger.

Cordelia screwed up her expression and moved toward where Bernard's hand rested. She pressed on the spot he was holding. He released it.

"What on earth?" Cordelia moved the spot around under her finger. She couldn't recall anything that would make a hard lump.

Bernard ran his hands over the center of the quilt. "There are others," he said as he pointed out another spot, and then another. Cordelia touched each spot in turn. Why hadn't she ever felt those before? Probably because the very center had been Grammy's handiwork and she had concentrated on the area outside of the circle.

Staring at the quilt brought a lot of thoughts to mind. Grammy's words . . . *Take care of your quilt, and it will take care of you.* Her work . . . neat and in concentric circles, while the work Cordelia and Gertie had done had been erratic and unorganized, not an even circle in any of it. Her attention went back to the lumps. She rose from the bed and opened her sewing box for the cuticle scissors. She hopped back on the bed and pulled the quilt onto her lap, displacing Bernard.

"What are you doing?" He moved closer.

"Well, whatever is in there needs to come out before it ruins the fabric. It's a good thing I didn't wash this or the wringer would have destroyed the material in these spots."

Cordelia carefully loosened the row of stitches holding each piece in place. She folded back the other triangles and gently pulled the last stitch from the first lump. As she released the last stitch and pulled on the triangle, a dark red ruby, the size of her thumbnail, slid out of the material.

Cordelia picked it up from the quilt. "What on earth?"

Bernard carefully took it from her fingers. "If I'm not mistaken, this is a ruby." He looked confused. "What is it doing in your quilt?"

Cordelia shook her head. "I don't have any idea. But if that's what was in here, what are all those?"

They both stared at the quilt.

33

July 15, 1955

Cordelia sat on the veranda rocking Camille in her arms. She had formulated a plan to start a Pinecone Quilt for her beloved four-month-old daughter. She looked down at the tiny hands and feet joyfully bobbing around. She brought the baby close for a hug that elicited a squeal of protest from the tiny person. A great smile spread across Cordelia's face.

She had plenty of time for Camille's quilt, years in fact, but it made her happy to think of her own precious quilt, all the love built into it, and passing on the family history.

It had been nine years since the rebirthing of their lives, as she liked to call it. Bernard came home from the war in October 1945, and the full sum of the next year was a real rebirth. It wasn't immediate, and there were still several years of trials and tribulations. But discovering her inheritance from Grammy the first year Bernard came home went a long way to healing the pains. There were many prayers over the years thanking the Lord for the blessing.

All in all, the quilt her grandmother had started for her had hidden rubies, star sapphires, a couple of large pearls, two diamond rings, and several gold coins. A dozen gems in all. The letter in Grammy's Bible made sense after the discovery.

Grammy had written it in sort of a code, Cordelia surmised, to keep other members of the family from figuring it out.

While not a windfall inheritance, it did afford them a modest nest egg, enough money to convince Stoney to sell the garage to Bernard. The change in Bernard was almost immediate. Once he felt self-worth again, he stopped drinking and turned the garage into a moneymaking business. The modest income allowed them to move out of the ramshackle house in the alley and into a cute little home on the Avenue. With Cordelia and Anna's help, Bernard made peace with his father, and eventually gave his dad a job in the garage. The two men found they worked well together, and it helped the business thrive.

Cordelia's heart warmed to see the two men getting along after being at odds for so many years. If she wanted any one thing to remember from her Grammy Mae, it was to look through people's pain to see who they really are.

The dark days of Bernard's battle fatigue behind them, Cordelia never shared the stress and pain outside of their home. It was their problem. Many women in her circles thought of her as a battered woman, and in many respects, she was. Night terrors when Bernard woke flailing about usually meant she'd have a black eye for a few days. But explaining his distress only meant embarrassing Bernard. People might think he couldn't handle what he had gone through in the war. The biggest drawback was that, since he never saw actual combat, other people thought he had had it easy. Within four years of coming home, six of the guys in his platoon had committed suicide.

Cordelia determined that Bernard was not going to be one of those statistics. She prayed over it every day. He still suffered from occasional nightmares, but Cordelia's love helped him cope with each new episode. She had become quite adept at handling the demons that tormented his spirit. He renewed his relationship with God. They found a new church where both he and his family could make a fresh start. The connection to church had proved fruitful.

Cordelia's skills as a clothing designer and master pattern maker allowed her to work from home, which pleased Bernard to no end, and now . . . they had a child.

God had fulfilled all of her dreams.

She pulled Camille close, cradled in the center of her Pinecone Quilt, and smiled.

God is faithful to answer all our prayers.

Discussion Questions

1. What effects can bullying have on children as they become adults? How can a fear of fighting or a reluctance to face confrontation affect a marriage?

2. What was your fairytale marriage scenario when you were a child?

3. How have you identified with friends who went to war and came back as a different person, or suffered from PTSD?

4. When you have problems or suffer blows that life has dealt you, how do you rationalize why these things happen to you?

5. How do you think a person should handle a spouse with PTSD when they know the person's actions aren't voluntary?

6. What steps would you take before divorce, especially in circumstances such as Bernard went through?

7. What effect do you think generations of men and women from WWII, the Korean Conflict, and Vietnam not getting relevant help with their battle fatigue has done to our nation?

8. What programs do you see or know of that offer mental and psychological help for our veterans coming home from Iraq or Afghanistan?

9. What kind of advice could you offer any woman who needs support for coping with this kind of wounded warrior?

10. Can you think of ways to be a blessing to someone suffering from the ravages of war?

11. What kind of mental and/or physical craft like quilting have you used to focus your emotions during a troubling time and then were able to display it as a time of victory in your life?

Note to Readers

Dear Reader,

I originally created this work as back story concerning my Sloane Templeton character in my first novel with Abingdon titled *Cooking the Books*. Sloane is a third-generation battered woman when her story begins but learns to overcome her circumstances. This story, *Pieces of the Heart*, is the story of Sloane's grandmother, Cordelia Grace, the first-generation battered woman in that family.

But Cordelia's story is not the typical story you would think of for a battered woman. She spends her whole life in love with one man, and the man who comes home from the war is just a shell of the man she loved. Her love and the quilt her grandmother created for her are the anchors that carry them through the stormy times and into the light at the end of the tunnel that leads back to God.

The centerpiece of this story is a traditional African American quilting pattern called the Pinecone Quilt, in some circles also called a Pine Burr Quilt. It was designated the official quilt of the State of Alabama by their legislature on March 11, 1997. There was a Pinecone Quilt in my family, but it was lost in the flooding of Wilkes Barre, Pennsylvania, during Hurricane Agnes in 1972.

Since there were no images available to use for this book cover, I recreated a copy of that quilt. Using scraps of reds, whites, and blues (to go with the war theme and the traditional scrap materials used for a quilt) I worked diligently. In the meantime Abingdon's art department came up with the perfect color scheme and an exact replica of the kitchen that I had in mind for the story. The only problem was that my quilt color scheme and Abingdon's color scheme were polar opposites. Thanks to the creative magic of electronic photo-shopping techniques, my sample quilt now has the correct colors on this cover!

As time has gone by, like the changing of the quilt colors to meet a higher expectation, the theme of this book has developed a larger meaning.

Although WWII was a sad time for our nation, it was also an awakening of sorts. Up until that time our military had a long-standing policy of segregation. Eleanor Roosevelt's airplane ride with Charles "Chief" Anderson of the first all-black air squadron called Tuskegee Airmen and, later in the war, the fame of the Red Ball Express both helped erase the inequality in our military. You can read many of these encounters in U.S. Department of Defense or National Archive websites.

Many of the incidents portrayed here in New Caledonia during the war were experiences of my late father. It took him many years to get over them and even to the end there were many things that were still too painful to discuss. WWII soldiers came home with battle fatigue, which we today call PTSD, and they were expected to "buck up and get over it." There was no medical or social help to the extent that we have available today.

Still today, as we end wars on several fronts, we are welcoming home thousands of brave men and women who are also going to suffer from PTSD. I pray to God that we, as a nation, do everything in our power to help these mentally and physically wounded warriors of this generation and their families.

Bonnie S. Calhoun

Want to learn more about author
Bonnie S. Calhoun and check out other great
fiction from Abingdon Press?

Sign up for our fiction newsletter at
www.AbingdonPress.com
to read interviews with your favorite authors, find tips
for starting a reading group, and stay posted on what
new titles are on the horizon. It's a place to connect
with other fiction readers or post a
comment about this book.

Be sure to visit Bonnie online!

www.bonniescalhoun.com

We hope you enjoyed *Pieces of the Heart* and that you will continue to read the Quilts of Love series of books from Abingdon Press. Here's an excerpt from the next book in the series, Carla Olson Gade's *Pattern for Romance.*

Pattern for Romance

Carla Olson Gade

1

Boston, Massachusetts
July 31, 1769

The crack of musket fire resounded through the clouded sky. Hailstones, the size of goose eggs, pelted the cobbled thoroughfare while people ran for shelter. Thunder clapped and an onslaught of shouts and shrieks echoed nature's vehement warning. Honour Metcalf sank to her knees in a puddle of quilted petticoats and toile—her mittened hands encasing her head, striving for protection against the artillery of hail and confusion.

"Miss Metcalf, Miss Metcalf . . ."

A muffled voice reached her ears and she dared peek at the one towering over her. Blue eyes—those eyes—flashed concern, then vanished as a dark cloak enveloped her. Strong arms scooped her up, pressing her against the firm chest of her rescuer.

Honour could scarcely make out the blur of damaged brick and clapboard as Joshua Sutton's long strides carried her away in haste. Glazed windows popped and shards of glass flew as the hail continued to wreak havoc on shops and offices. Fallen birds littered the street amidst the frozen ammunition. Lightning flashed and Honour squeezed her eyes shut, willing away the shrill neighs of horses and the cracking of the hail beneath carriage wheels.

At last, the pair made their way through a heavy wooden door and into a dimly lit foyer. Mr. Sutton rested Honour upon a long bench and stooped beside her. With trembling hands, she pushed back her taffeta calash. The boned collapsible bonnet had provided some measure of protection from the torrent, but what would protect her from him?

"How do you fare, Miss Metcalf?" Mr. Sutton asked.

Honour's heart pounded, much the same as she had felt Mr. Sutton's while she had hovered against his chest. Her eyes darted around the room before her frightened gaze locked on his. Darkened and dampened by the storm, his hair spread wildly about his shoulders, his ocean blue eyes awaiting her answer.

"Miss Metcalf. I asked if you are well."

The edge in his voice lifted her out of the fog and she rubbed her temple. "Mr. Sutton? Aye, I am well enough. Where . . . why are we here?" Honour glanced at the small leaded glass window, a piece of golden glass missing from a corner and other sections cracked.

"I found you in the street getting pummeled by hailstones. I brought you here to the meeting house for shelter." Thunder rolled again and Mr. Sutton's eyes shot toward the door.

"How long will it last?" Her young sister was safe at the dame school, or so she hoped.

"That, only the Almighty knows." He surveyed her as if assessing a length of cloth. "Are you certain you are uninjured, Miss Metcalf?"

"I am . . . I must go." She attempted to rise, but sat back as a wave of dizziness overcame her.

"Please rest for a moment. You cannot go back out there." His mouth drew into a line. "Perhaps we should pray."

"Surely I did, as you carried me here." She felt a warm blush rise on her neck. Never had she been in such intimate proximity to a man while in his arms. And never had she dreamt of being so near Mr. Sutton, certainly not today.

"And I prayed, as well. Then we shall trust the good Lord for the outcome, shall we? After all, we have found refuge in His house." Mr. Sutton smiled and the corners of his eyes crinkled with reassurance.

Honour replied with a simple nod and regarded his kind face. "It is you who are injured, Mr. Sutton." She extended her hand toward his bruised cheek, and then retreated.

He instinctively found the bruise on his cheekbone, then felt his temple. A trickle of blood mixed with rainwater streamed down the side of his face. He looked at the blood on his hand and shrugged. "'Tis nothing. Perhaps a little feverfew tea will help."

"You might as well have been lambasted by rocks at the hands of town delinquents. If your head hurts, as mine is beginning to, it will take more than tea, I fear."

"The tea would warm me more. It hurts me little." The corner of his mouth curved.

"This is no time for mirth, Mr. Sutton," Honour said, as she searched for her satchel. "I would offer you a handkerchief, but I've none in my pocket and cannot seem to find my workbag. I must have dropped it in the road."

Mr. Sutton gestured toward her cloak pocket. "May I?"

Only then did Honour notice his greatcoat draped awkwardly around her shoulders, her own short chintz cape beneath, which she had hastily donned, perchance it rained. He must have wrapped his cloak over her when he whisked her away from the harsh elements—including the British officers. When they'd come rushing toward her, she'd crumbled to the ground, and her legs turned to porridge despite her urge to flee. But the dark sky and giant balls of ice caused her to succumb to nature's assault. Like the fire and brimstone punishment of the ancients, God had thrown down water and ice to execute judgment upon her.

She attempted to remove the coat, but he stayed her hand with his. Though cold, his firm, yet gentle clasp exuded the warmth of one who cared. Or was it her mere imagination? Her heart dared not hope.

"No. You need it for warmth. One would scarcely know 'tis a summer day." He retrieved a handkerchief from his coat and wiped at his cut. He refolded the linen cloth and placed it inside a pocket of his damp-about-the-shoulders waistcoat. "Now tell me of this satchel of yours. Is it of great importance?"

She worried her lip and nodded.

"Perhaps we can yet find it. If not, you might obtain a new one from my father's store, if you'd allow me to replace it."

Honour wrinkled her brow. "Though I do appreciate your offer, Mr. Sutton, it must be found. 'tis not only my workbag, but of special value to me. It was a gift from my late mother."

"Let us hope, then, it may be retrieved . . . once the storm has passed." He glanced upward to the high ceiling of the vestibule, and her gaze followed—the hail continuing to pound the slate roof of the church in an unnerving staccato.

"Yes, I do hope. My mother taught me to quilt and the embroidered bag once belonged to her. It is very dear to me, indeed, as far as material things. Though I do hope I do not sound selfish to talk of such a small matter while people may yet be out there injured from the storm and dealing with the damage to their buildings." She rubbed the base of her skull, the dull ache intensifying, yet she wished not to concern Mr. Sutton.

The man grinned, and a darling crease appeared by his mouth. "I do not think there is one thimbleful of selfishness inside you, Miss Metcalf."

"Then you do not know me well enough, Mr. Sutton." Honour smiled shyly and lowered her gaze, her heavy lids beckoning her to succumb to the drowsy feeling tugging at her.

"Perhaps we may remedy that somehow."

"Mmm." Her eyes grew leaden as an aura of slumber descended upon her.

"Miss Metcalf!"

Honour's head bobbed up. "Yes?" She felt as though she were floating in the ocean—submerging one moment, and above a wave another.

Joshua Sutton still knelt before her, his eyes stayed on hers, as if he could hold her up by sheer will. Then he peered down at her skirts, to her quilted outer petticoat. Aye, she'd worn her favorite blue silk quilt today, with her blue and yellow toile polonaise gown. Did he find her attractive? She felt her damp skirt. Mercy, she must look like a shipwreck.

"Your quilt, Miss Metcalf. It is sublime. Is it your own hand-iwork?" he asked.

"Yes, thank you," she said softly, trying to remain alert, just as he seemed to be attempting to keep her so. "I learned from my mother. There was never a finer quilter than she."

"I have heard you are an adept quilter, but I have never seen evidence of it until now. Your mother taught you well. Perhaps my father can make use of your services for banyans and waistcoats and such, since we can no longer obtain quilted cloth from England."

Honour stared through him, her vision blurring him into two.

"Dare I say, it is a pity your hem got wet . . . Miss Metcalf, are you listening?"

Honour leaned over to inspect the hemline of her petticoat. But instead of seeing the quilted cloth, she found darkness, as the sound of hail and Mr. Sutton's smooth voice faded into nothingness.

⸺⸻⸺

"Who goes there?"

Joshua recognized the deep baritone voice at once. He looked up as the parson entered through the vestry doors, only to greet him with Miss Metcalf slumped against his chest and gripping her shoulders. "Reverend Cooper, I have come to seek shelter for the lady and myself, though she just now seems to have swooned."

Lantern in hand, the reverend's eyes widened as he came near. "Good heavens . . ."

"Please help me lay her on the bench. She was battered much by the hailstorm and it seems to have done her in."

"Why, of course." The parson set the lantern on a small table and shuffled over to help.

After laying her down, Joshua stood and faced the minister. "Thank you, sir." Joshua had never seen this man of the cloth in such disarray—without his powdered bob wig and crisp black suit. Instead, he wore breeches and a plain linsey-woolsey waistcoat.

Reverend Cooper seemed to become aware of his disheveled state. "You must forgive my appearance. When there was a short reprieve from the storm I went out and about to assess the damage to the church, as the sexton is away, then it started up again and soaked me through."

Reverend Cooper swiped an errant lock of hair into place over his balding head, and replaced his cap. "Now what happened to the young lady? And who is she, pray tell?"

"I found her collapsed in the street being accosted by the hail. A few British officers were about to give her aid at the same time I arrived. They asked if I knew her. I told them that I recognized her as Miss Honour Metcalf, an employee of Mrs. Wadsworth, the mantua maker. Before I could say more the officers fled to help others."

"Mmmhmph." Reverend Cooper's brow wrinkled with concern. He pursed his lips and signaled Joshua to continue.

"Most of the shopkeepers have locked their doors in the chaos and we were far from our own. I was greatly relieved to find refuge here," Joshua said.

Reverend Cooper clamped his index finger across his jaw. "Rather fitting, I say, to find a safe haven in the house of the Lord, especially when such mysterious elements from heaven descend."

Joshua released a slow breath. "Indeed it is."

The reverend's wiry eyebrows twitched. "Though I suspect you are not entirely comfortable here."

"Not entirely, sir."

The minister nodded, "You are Joshua Sutton, the tailor's son, are you not?"

"Yes, Reverend, I am."

"And how well do you know this young lady?"

"I am only briefly acquainted with her, as Sutton's Clothiers and Wadsworth's Mantua Shop have occasion to do business with one another. But we are not attached, if that is what you are asking." An embarrassed grin formed on Joshua's lips and he shook his head in denial. He had no interest whatsoever in becoming attached to any lady, whether from here in Boston to as far as the West Indies. Even if she was as lovely as Miss Metcalf.

The man cocked his head and arched an eyebrow. "Well, perhaps you should consider it."

Was the reverend jesting or accusing? Joshua swallowed. "Pardon me, sir, but I am uncertain of your implication. I assure you it is as I said. My only intent was for her well-being. Would you have me marry her simply because you found me here alone with her? I assure you it is entirely innocent."

The man issued a sardonic grin. "It is why some young couples seek me out mid-week. In fact, I wed a young couple this morning at the home of Widow Lankton. Her niece, you know. I understand you are acquainted."

Joshua grimaced.

"Pardon me, son. Perhaps I should have refrained from mentioning it. But I thought it would be of particular interest to you. You must be relieved to see her settled."

Joshua clenched his jaw and stared at the stone floor. It should have been he who wed Emily Guilfold. But now, his name was marred, and her reputation sullied, despite her attempt to "settle." Though she did not confess her sin, some assumed. Why else would she marry Leach so soon after she had broken off their own attachment? And because of it some said Joshua had also been inappropriately engaged with her. He hoped the gossip would abate until matters could be set straight. A good enough reason to refrain from going to the taverns for a while—and mayhap Sunday meeting. Though Mother would tan his hide if he was absent from their family pew.

"Yes, Miss Guilfold informed me she was to marry by special license. Though I did not know the marriage was to occur this day."

"Mistress Leach, now," the minister said. "By all appearances the couple seemed to wed in haste, but you may put yourself at ease. Widow Lankton assured me it was for the best, though I am not at liberty to discuss it in detail."

Why must the old man ramble on so? Joshua's character was blemished; he did not need to dwell on it. Nor did he wish to hear about "Mrs. Leach."

A soft groan came from Miss Metcalf and the two pivoted in her direction. Joshua would deal with his irreverent thoughts later.

"Does she need an apothecary? A physician perhaps?" Reverend Cooper asked.

"I suppose that she does." Joshua went to the door and pushed it ajar against the pressure of the wind. Ice pellets continued to come down, now mixed with rain. He hoped it would subside soon. "I should go for Dr. Westcott."

"I have seen storms as this in my lifetime. You should not go out again until the torrent ceases. I fear it may continue for some time," the clergyman said.

Joshua shut the door. "But what of Miss Metcalf? I tried to keep her awake by talking, as I feared she might've obtained a concussion." Joshua glanced at her still form. "Perhaps we should try to wake her."

"Sleep might be best for now, son. At least, until the storm has passed."

Miss Metcalf murmured unintelligible words. The men shifted their attention toward her, and then the reverend bowed his head. While Reverend Cooper entreated the Lord in silence, Joshua knelt by her side. He cast aside his own misery, as a strong desire to stroke her deep auburn locks and calm away her fears emerged from some place deep within.

He brushed a loose tendril from her pallid face. "Hush now, all is well."

"Joshua?"

Reverend Cooper cleared his throat following a quiet "Amen."

Joshua withdrew his hand. He would not allow himself to succumb to such feelings again, even if he were the one to initiate them.

Yet, as the beauty slipped into unconsciousness once more, it occurred to him that she had called him by his Christian name, Joshua. Worse yet, he in turn addressed her with her own. Honour. Sweet, talented, and lovely Honour. Everything the beguiling Miss Guil—Mrs. Leach—was not.

QUILTS of LOVE

EVERY QUILT HAS A STORY

There is a strong connection between storytelling and quilts. Like a favorite recollection, quilts are passed from one generation to the next as precious heirlooms. They bring communities together.

The Quilts of Love series focuses on women who have woven romance, adventure, and even a little intrigue into their own family histories. Featuring contemporary and historical romances as well as occasional light mystery, this series will draw you into uplifting, heartwarming, exciting stories of characters you won't soon forget.

Visit **QuiltsofLoveBooks.com** for more information.

For more information and for more
fiction titles, please visit
AbingdonPress.com/fiction.

Abingdon Press fiction
a novel approach to faith

Plan your escape.

What They're Saying About...

The Glory of Green, by Judy Christie
"Once again, Christie draws her readers into the town, the life, the humor, and the drama in Green. *The Glory of Green* is a wonderful narrative of small-town America, pulling together in tragedy. A great read!"
—Ane Mulligan, editor of *Novel Journey*

Always the Baker, Never the Bride, by Sandra Bricker
"[It] had just the right touch of humor, and I loved the characters. Emma Rae is a character who will stay with me. Highly recommended!"
—Colleen Coble, author of *The Lightkeeper's Daughter* and the *Rock Harbor* series

Diagnosis Death, by Richard Mabry
"Realistic medical flavor graces a story rich with characters I loved and with enough twists and turns to keep the sleuth in me off-center. Keep 'em coming!"—**Dr. Harry Krauss, author of *Salty Like Blood* and *The Six-Liter Club***

Sweet Baklava, by Debby Mayne
"A sweet romance, a feel-good ending, and a surprise cache of yummy Greek recipes at the book's end? I'm sold!"—**Trish Perry, author of *Unforgettable* and *Tea for Two***

The Dead Saint, by Marilyn Brown Oden
"An intriguing story of international espionage with just the right amount of inspirational seasoning."—*Fresh Fiction*

Shrouded in Silence, by Robert L. Wise
"It's a story fraught with death, danger, and deception—of never knowing whom to trust, and with a twist of an ending I didn't see coming. Great read!"—Sharon Sala, author of *The Searcher's Trilogy: Blood Stains, Blood Ties,* and *Blood Trails.*

Delivered with Love, by Sherry Kyle
"Sherry Kyle has created an engaging story of forgiveness, sweet romance, and faith reawakened—and I looked forward to every page. A fun and charming debut!"—Julie Carobini, author of *A Shore Thing* and *Fade to Blue.*

Abingdon Press fiction
a novel approach to faith

AbingdonPress.com | 800.251.3320